CRITICAL ACCLAIM FOR ORPHAN ROAD

"*Orphan Road* is a breakneck tale of robbery and vengeance, as lyrical and gritty as a Bad Seeds tune. Superb."
—Sam Wiebe, award-winning author
of *Sunset and Jericho* and *Invisible Dead*

"*Orphan Road* hits *Mr Inbetween* levels of brilliance. Stylish writing and whip-smart dialogue, this is noir done right."
—David Whish-Wilson, author
of *Line of Sight* and *The Sawdust House*

"I have been waiting for another Gary Chance book. *Orphan Road* is grimy, twisty and fast. Absolutely worth the wait."
—Iain Ryan, author of *Four Days* and *The Student*

"A multi-continental heist romp, Nette's *Orphan Road* is in direct lineage with Westlake/Stark's Parker series and Thompson's *The Getaway*. Filled with pulpy goodness, this crime caper scratches your thieving itch. For fans of Barry Gifford's Black Lizard catalog, this one's a guaranteed delight."
—Nolan Knight, author of
The Neon Lights Are Veins and *Gallows Dome*

"Some people will do anything for money...or in this case diamonds. Gary Chance is one of those people and in *Orphan Road*, Andrew Nette gifts us with a good, old-fashioned hard-boiled thriller that moves at a machine-gun-like pace leaving the reader gasping for air."
—Charles Salzberg,
multiple Shamus Award-nominated author

ORPHAN ROAD

BOOKS BY ANDREW NETTE

Ghost Money
Gunshine State
Orphan Road

As Co-Editor
Girl Gangs, Biker Boys, and Real Cool Cats:
Pulp Fiction and Youth Culture, 1950 to 1980
Sticking it to the Man: Revolution and Counterculture
in Pulp and Popular Fiction, 1950-1980
Dangerous Visions and New Worlds: Radical
Science Fiction, 1950-1985

ANDREW NETTE

ORPHAN ROAD
A CHANCE NOVEL

Down & Out Books
3959 Van Dyke Road, Suite 265
Lutz, FL 33558
DownAndOutBooks.com

Orphan Road is a work of fiction. The central crime that inspired it, the 1976 Great Bookie Robbery and its aftermath, was real but all other characters, events and incidents depicted in this work are wholly imaginary. Any similarity to real persons, living or dead, is coincidental and not intended by the author.

Cover design by JT Lindroos

ISBN: 1-64396-315-5
ISBN-13: 978-1-64396-315-0

For Natasha

CHASING ATLANTIS

ONE

Chance ignored the pain gathering force in the back of his skull, concentrated on aping the same expression of joyous ecstasy on the faces of the surrounding cult members.

The young woman next to him, Shannon, a whippet-thin former legal secretary from Sydney, squeezed his arm, smiled as she swayed. Chance grinned back, swept her up in his arms in what he hoped would be interpreted as a gesture of abandon. She hugged back harder.

Around a hundred people occupied the circle of cleared forest that served as the venue for Cornelius's regular soul cleansing sessions. Chance battled his headache for the name of tonight's subject. Wetzler. A stockbroker in his mid-forties. Wetzler sat on the ground, Cornelius squatting behind him, holding the overweight man's arms as if helping him to give birth.

Tonight, Cornelius claimed to be channelling the spirit of Siphon, a nine-thousand-year-old Atlantean wizard. The cult leader's deep voice was audible above the new age synthesiser music blaring from speakers affixed like beehives to trees around the clearing. Tears streamed down Wetzler's chubby face as the crowd chanted at him to confess his spiritual impurities.

Chance had to hand it to Cornelius. He knew all the tricks: switching between abuse and intimacy, subliminal messaging. In another life, he would've excelled as an army interrogator, like the ones Chance had met during his tour in Afghanistan. The setting helped, the middle of the forest "to bring us closer to the spirit world," as Cornelius put it. A brilliant yellow moon partly obscured by wisps of cloud, a roaring log fire casting flickering shadows across the crowd as it shrieked and moved in time to the music.

When Tremont had first suggested robbing a cult, Chance imagined something like the Manson clan or a bunch of back-woods Christians who stockpiled guns and slept with each other's wives. New Atlantis was more like a rave party meets *Lord of the Flies*.

Chance broke away from Shannon's embrace, scanned the crowd. What he wouldn't give for a cigarette. Smokes were one of the many items forbidden by Cornelius because they made the human body unsuitable for re-occupation by the Atlanteans, who, according to him, would soon emerge from their home deep in the ocean to reclaim the planet.

Cornelius didn't exactly come across as prime real estate for a returning Atlantean spirit. Clad in a faded denim shirt and black jeans, eyes hidden by ever-present dark sunglasses, he struck Chance as a cut-price Jim Morrison, all bone and sinew, his skin stretched tight and weather-beaten. Chance watched Cornelius and wondered how many back roads and dingy motel rooms the cult leader had spent time in on the way to his current scam.

But Lilith was something else. Chance could well imagine an Atlantean spirit being at home in her form. She was one of the group's 'Elders', and watching Lilith was one of the few pleasures in New Atlantis not forbidden. She was in her late thirties, if the faint wisps of grey in her shoulder length black hair were any indication. Her mullet-style cut framed a lean, hungry face and sharp green eyes. She wore narrow-cut black cotton pants that showed off the contour of her strong legs, and a loose purple overshirt, its thin cotton accentuating her cleavage. Her suntanned skin looked caramel in the firelight.

Chance gripped the little finger of his left hand. The digit, taken off at the knuckle with a pair of garden shears years ago, had been replaced with one of his toes by a plastic surgeon in Thailand. Conscious of playing with it whenever he was nervous, he suddenly let go, worried he was giving himself away.

Lilith met Chance's gaze, held it. Chance felt a sharpness in his gut at the possibility she was onto him. Without taking her eyes from him, she inclined her head, said something to the bald man next to her. Swain, another Elder. A tall slab of a man, Chance wondered what the Atlanteans would make of the white supremacist tattoos that flowed out from under the sleeves of the black T-shirts he always wore and down his muscular arms.

A cry drew Chance's attention back to the centre of the clearing. Wetzler had broken. Head nestled against Cornelius's chest, he blubbered out his spiritual impurities: a selfish material life, fucking his secretary, tax evasion. Cornelius stroked Wetzler's thinning hair, leaned close, whispered in the man's ear. The stockbroker immediately became calm, his eyes fixed on a far point in the night sky only he could see.

The music stopped, signaling the ceremony was over. The cult members paused, shuffled on the spot like a crowd at a pub gig when the lights come on, reluctant for the night to end. Chance joined them as they drifted towards the dormitories, watching from the corner of his eye as Cornelius and Lilith led Wetzler in the opposite direction. Chance knew from Tremont they always followed a soul cleansing by a one-on-one debrief during which Cornelius counselled the individual concerned about the uselessness of worldly possessions, now they had reached a heightened stage of spiritual consciousness. They met resistance with hints about what would happen if the information the subject had divulged fell into the wrong hands.

At first sight of the dormitories, Chance ducked behind a large gum tree. He waited until the last of the crowd had filed inside and made his way around the perimeter of the compound, pausing now and again to make sure he was alone. He found the spot he was looking for, scooped away the dirt, unearthed the zip-lock plastic bag he'd buried soon after arriving in New Atlantis. The bag contained a stainless-steel wristwatch and a flashlight. Two more items banned in New Atlantis. He peered at the tiny green dots on the dial. Ten forty-five. Tremont would wait until two a.m.

Cornelius lived in an old wooden farmhouse on the property. The door was unlocked, the threat of expulsion for anyone caught near the house, the only security Cornelius needed. Chance whistled softly as the torch beam moved across the main living area. Sleek metal and leather furniture competed for attention with Asian-themed wall hangings, rugs and throws. A large plasma screen television stood against one wall, a well-stocked liquor cabinet by another.

The trap door was under a rug in the bedroom, exactly where Tremont had said. Chance pulled the latch, put a hand in, felt smooth, cool wood, but nothing else. He withdrew his hand as though he'd received an electric shock.

The money was gone.

Chance crouched in the darkness. The hairs on his arms and neck bristled. Had Tremont double crossed him? There was no way his partner might have made it onto the property and stolen the money without being detected. That left two other possibilities. Tremont's information was wrong or someone else had taken it.

He stood up, only to be immediately thrown back to the ground. The circle of light from the dropped torch illuminated a booted foot, the rest of his assailant a grunting shadow.

He wrestled with the figure. A blow cut deep into Chance's upper lip. Fireworks went off in his vision and his mouth filled with the taste of his own blood. His assailant used the seconds while Chance recovered to roll on top of him and try to pin him to the ground.

Chance threw several punches. Most found only air, one connected. A wet crack that was his fist, finding what felt like his assailant's nose. Chance tried to leverage himself up, but a blow snapped his head back onto the wooden floorboards.

The pain became more distant with each blow, until he felt nothing.

Chance's last job, working a long-haul prawn trawler out of Cairns, had seemed an ideal way to avoid the authorities. At first, he'd welcomed being at sea, no external contact except a tanker which delivered food and fuel and took away the catch. Until he got to know the crew: a captain whose idea of letting off steam was to fire a shotgun at sharks trying to get the catch; a deckhand who got his kicks playing practical jokes with the chemicals used to freeze the prawns; another whose standard reply to anything was 'What happens on the boat, stays on the boat.'

But the worst part was going through the nets. You had to sort the prawns without gloves to feel for the soft and broken ones. He still had scars all over his hands from the cuts. Not to mention the various lethal creatures that got caught in the catch. All of them had either a ferocious attack or defence mechanism. Or both.

The first opportunity, Chance split, made his way to the New South Wales town of Byron Bay. He'd been there two weeks, waiting on a call from a man named Loomis. A cut out for Vera Leigh, Loomis dealt with anything messy or illegal, which in Leigh's business—owning one of Melbourne's best-regarded S&M dungeons with a sideline acting as a message service for criminals and people wanting to employ them—kept him busy. He mediated disputes, connected people with jobs, ensured Leigh took a cut of everything he helped put together.

When Loomis's call finally came, the faintly British voice gave him contact details for a Carl Tremont. Chance met Tremont in a backpacker bar in the middle of town. Tremont came across as a middle-aged hustler, heavily tanned skin, black hair tied in a ponytail, his white shirt unbuttoned to reveal a chunky Buddha amulet on a gold chain around his neck. A self-described cult buster, Tremont had set up shop a decade earlier in Byron Bay, a place where the hardcore remnants of the seventies counter-culture faced off against pastoralists, hard-core Bible thumpers, and, in the last few years, an influx of monied celebrities and social media influencers.

On their second meeting, Tremont was accompanied by Celeste, a curvy, animated woman with a head of frizzy ginger hair. After drinking for a couple of hours, the three of them ended up on an L-shaped black leather couch in the family suite of the motor court Tremont called home.

'I know it's not much, but it's the best I could do given the shortage of accommodation in Byron,' said Tremont, looking around the room and shaking his head. 'Not so bad once you get used to it.'

Celeste chopped up lines of coke on a glass coffee table, eighties stadium rock low on the stereo, while the cult buster told Chance about New Atlantis, a hundred-hectare property cut out of rainforest near the town of Mullumbimby, north of Byron.

'Established by a bloke called Terry Cornelius. Claims he can channel the spirits of Atlantean wizards who died when their city was wiped out by an alien invasion thousands of years ago.

'He preaches humanity is simply a transitory stage, that we're merely minding our bodies until the Atlanteans return to reclaim them.' As Tremont spoke, Celeste did a line. 'The faithful will be elevated to a higher level of existence while the rest of humanity is destroyed. Something like that.'

'And people actually believe this shit?' said Chance.

Celeste paused mid-snort, shot Chance a wounded look. 'It's not shit, Gary.'

'Celeste, not now,' said Tremont with a tight smile.

'Carl, baby, just saying, what Cornelius preaches about us simply being the keepers of our bodies until the Atlanteans return, it's not all—'

'Honey, I get it, but not now. Okay?'

Celeste pouted silently.

Tremont put a hand on her shoulder. 'Would you go get Gary another beer, love?'

He shook his head, looked to the ceiling after she'd gone. 'Nice lady, great in the sack, but a half a sandwich short of a picnic, if you know what I mean.' He winked at Chance. 'It's the same with a lot of cult survivors. The experience leaves them a little mixed up.'

Chance glanced in the direction of the kitchen, then back at Tremont, his eyebrows raised.

'Her old man paid me five grand to get her out of New Atlantis. Our contract didn't say nothing about what would happen afterwards.' Tremont shrugged, flashed Chance a sly grin. 'Besides, as you can see, I still have a bit of deprogramming work to do on her.

'Anyway, Celeste was Cornelius's missus for a time, and he was real open with the pillow talk, all the details of his operation, including where he stashes his money.'

Tremont leant forward, did a line, pinched his nose, and indicated for Chance to do the same. Chance shook his head, rolled a cigarette.

'Don't worry, Gary, the coke is for down time only,' said Tremont, noting the look of disapproval on Chance's face. 'I'm always clean when I work.'

Tremont sat back, stretched his arms in either direction along the top of the couch, sniffed, swiped his forearm under his nose. 'New Atlantis has all the features associated with your garden-variety, nut job cult. Isolationist. Obsessed with the end of the world. Run along strict hierarchical lines, etcetera. But while the foot soldiers grow organic vegetables, those who've been spiritually purged and are loyal to Cornelius have a higher calling, tending the high-grade ganja he sells to dealers along the northern NSW coast.

'Their product is good, and it's a cash business. And being crazy, Cornelius doesn't trust banks. It's April, growing season's almost over and I hear they've sold most of the latest crop.'

Tremont rubbed his hands together. 'Now does that sound like a sweet deal or does that sound like a sweet deal?'

Chance fired up his rollie from a novelty hand grenade lighter on the table, thought about the mechanics of the job, energised by the prospect of working again.

'What about security?'

'A couple of heavies to keep the local rednecks at bay.'

'If the money is so lightly guarded, there's nothing to stop us from going in and getting it, right?'

'No. Guys like Cornelius are conditioned to expect someone to come at them from outside, cops or a rival grower.'

'Or someone like you.'

'Correct. But he'd never expect trouble from within. Believe me, I know what I'm talking about. I've been dealing with people like him for years.' Tremont looked around the motel room, sighed. 'With the money from this score I can get out of this dead-end game, do something else.'

'So, what's your plan?'

Celeste returned, passed a can of beer to Chance. Tremont put an arm around her waist, smiled up at her. 'Celeste, baby, tell Gary about life in New Atlantis.'

The New Atlantis minivan came into Mullumbimby for supplies every few days. It wasn't hard to spot. Tremont told him to look for a vehicle with what had supposedly been the traditional symbol of Atlantis, a cross in concentric circles.

Chance tried striking up a conversation with the driver, an older woman in a faded rainbow coloured caftan called Connie. He told her he was an ex-independent contractor gone bust, fresh from a bad divorce, depressed, looking for a different path.

When that didn't get him anywhere, he disabled the van's clutch sensor while Connie was shopping for supplies, then offered to fix it when she returned and couldn't start the engine. Lilith accompanied Connie on her next visit, asked Chance whether he was interested in coming out to have a look at New Atlantis. On his second visit, they invited him to stay.

Chance rang Tremont before he left, made a plan to meet him, with the money, in seven days.

The first thing Chance felt was pain. He remembered the beating, then he noticed the smell, a cloying organic aroma.

He was cheek down on a rough wooden floor, four sets of feet at eye level. He inclined his head. Lilith, Cornelius, Swain, another man, short, broad shouldered with a head of blonde hair, were all backlit by a single globe hanging from a corrugated iron ceiling. Short Man glared at Chance, dabbed his fingers at the dried blood around his nostrils. Cornelius was dressed in the same clothes he'd been wearing at the soul cleansing, but Lilith had changed into old boots, jeans, and a faded red cowboy shirt.

Cornelius nodded and Swain and the Short Man lifted Chance off the ground and sat him roughly into a wooden chair. Short Man propped him up, dug his strong fingers hard into Chance's shoulder while Swain tied a plastic rope around him, smiled as Chance winced. When they were finished, the two men resumed their position on either side of the cult leader.

The walls were lined with tinfoil, plastic chemical containers stacked against one wall. In the doorway behind his captors hung a row of drying marijuana plants. Chance's eyes came to a standstill on a metal workbench where a selection of knives lay neatly arranged on top of an unfolded black canvas pouch, alongside a metal cylinder that looked horribly like a blowtorch.

Cornelius adjusted his dark sunglasses, ran boney fingers through his hair.

'Where's my fucking money?' he said. Stripped of the theatrics, his voice had a brutal, authoritative tone.

'It was already gone when I got there.' Chance heard his own voice waver.

'Figured as much.' Cornelius scratched at the stubble on his face. 'No sense you stealing the money and coming back to an empty cubbyhole. But the thing is...' he lost his train of thought, looked at Lilith. 'What's this guy's name again?'

'Bell. Lawrence Bell.'

'The thing is, Mister Bell, you were trying to steal it all the same. You must know something, follow my meaning?'

'Maybe he's a jack,' spat Short Man.

'Shut up, Dobbs.' Cornelius flashed his enforcer an annoyed look as he picked up the metal cylinder from the workbench, twisted a valve at one end of it. There was a hiss, and a tongue of blue flame came to life.

'You must be a pretty crappy messiah to resort to something as old-fashioned as a blowtorch to get answers.' Chance tried to sound braver than he felt.

'Don't be disappointed, son.' Cornelius's smile exposed two rows of uneven yellow teeth. 'There's so many people claiming to be something in this world they're not. Jesus, Satan or whoever. People lining up to believe them. Way it's always been. Way it always will be.'

'Sounds like you've been smoking too much of your own product.'

'Never touch the stuff.' Cornelius brought the flame close to Chance, ran it close to his bare arm, and took it away. Chance flinched at the proximity of the purring heat, focused on trying to control his bowels. The smell of burning hair mixed with the aroma of the drying marijuana.

'I'm working with someone on the outside,' Chance said quickly. 'A man called Tremont.' He noticed Cornelius's brow furrow at the mention of the name. 'He gets people out of places like this. One of them told him about the money.'

Chance looked at Lilith as he spoke. She gazed back at him, her face blank.

'He hatched the plan, recruited me to work it from the inside. I was supposed to steal the money, meet him at the front entrance at midnight.'

'Swain, Dobbs, take the van, go and pick up Tremont. Do it quietly. Don't wake the sheep.' Cornelius stared at Chance as he spoke. His glasses reflected the flame from the blowtorch. 'Bring him back here,' he yelled after them. 'Alive.'

Within moments of the men leaving, Chance heard a vehicle splutter into life, drive off.

'Now, what to do with you, Mister Bell?'

Lilith stepped towards the workbench, picked up a short bladed knife. 'Terry, I reckon I can think of something,' she said, her voice husky.

She stood next to Cornelius, held the knife in front of his face.

The cult leader smiled, licked his upper lip. 'You're full of surprises, ain't you, baby?' He turned off the blowtorch.

With a quick movement, Lilith slashed the knife across Cornelius's throat, stepped back. Blood poured through Cornelius's fingers as he clutched helplessly at the cut. He swayed like one of his followers during a spiritual cleansing, fell backwards onto the ground, squirmed a few moments and was still.

Lilith stared at the body, eyes bulging, her breath short gasps. She shook her head hard, glanced at Chance as if noticing him for the first time.

'Whoever you are, we've got to move quickly,' she said, cutting the plastic binding around him. Chance stood, rubbed his wrists for a moment, grabbed Lilith's knife hand by the wrist, twisted it behind her back, put his other arm around her neck.

Lilith dropped the knife and yelped in pain. 'What the—'

'I don't know what the hell is in the water around here,' hissed Chance, 'but before we go anywhere, I want some answers.'

'You're hurting me.'

Chance twisted her arm further.

'Okay, okay,' she stopped struggling. 'I stole the money.' She uttered a gritty laugh at Chance's silence. 'What, upset I crashed your little party?' Her voice had regained its confidence.

Chance cursed, let her go. 'How much?'

'I haven't had the chance to count it, but enough.'

'Now you got a partner.'

Her green eyes glared at him. 'Why the hell should I throw my lot in with you when your last partner is probably having his teeth kicked out by Swain and Dobbs as we speak.'

'I'm not the one who just killed a man.'

'Believe me, mate, that wasn't originally on tonight's agenda. Odds were when Cornelius had finished with you, he would've looked elsewhere for suspects and eventually settled on me. Anyway, I could've left you here, let Cornelius slowly barbecue you.'

'And I appreciate you not doing that,' he said, staring at Cornelius, who lay face up, surrounded by a balloon of dark liquid. His sunglasses had slipped off, the whites of his eyes staring up into his skull.

'Besides, my partner's safe for now. Unless Cornelius's thugs went in the opposite direction to the one I gave them.' Chance scanned the room as he spoke, fixed on a pile of tools on the floor. He stepped carefully around the blood, selected a large spanner, tested it for heft.

He glanced at his watch. Less than an hour to get the money and meet Tremont. He quickly explained the plan to Lilith.

'Now where's the money?'

Her brow furrowed as she weighed up her options.

'Don't piss around,' Chance snapped. 'The money, where is it?'

'I hid it.'

Chance fought a wave of exhaustion. His face throbbed. 'Where?'

'Behind the farmhouse.'

The night was clouding over, and a wind had whipped up. Chance listened to the foliage rustling in the trees above him as he crouched impatiently in bushes near the farmhouse. Lilith had been gone almost fifteen minutes. He turned the spanner over in his hands, wondered whether he'd been an idiot to trust her, another criminal. He was weighing up what the odds were she'd retrieved the money and run when he heard a movement in the bushes to his right.

'Lilith?' he whispered.

Without a word, a figure stepped towards him. Its shape wasn't right, shorter and thicker. A man. Chance didn't hesitate, lunged towards the figure, swung the spanner as he moved. The man went down. Chance hit him again as he lay on the ground to make sure. He peered at the body, recognised Dobbs.

'Got it,' came a female voice behind him. Chance, his mind racing and blood simple, twisted around, raised the spanner, ready to strike.

'Whoa, boy, it's me.' She raised one hand palm out towards him. The other clutched a canvas bag. She noticed the body on the ground.

'Dobbs.'

Chance breathed deeply, nodded.

'Is he...?'

'Dead? I don't know and don't have time to find out.'

He took the bag, unzipped it, looked inside. Twenty- and fifty-dollar notes, some tied with rubber bands, the rest loose. Nowhere near the million Tremont had promised, but at least he wouldn't walk out of the job with nothing. He zipped the bag shut, slung it across his shoulder.

'Who nominated you for bag duty?'

Chance glared at her, started walking.

They ducked and weaved through the thick undergrowth that surrounded the New Atlantis compound, emerging onto a flat stretch of pasture. The moon was now almost completely covered in cloud, the wind stronger and pregnant with the smell of impending rain.

'Has anyone told you your timing sucks?' she said as they walked.

'All the time.'

'Two fucking months, pretending to chase Atlantis with the rest of the crazies, trying to keep Cornelius's paws off me long enough to score the cash and get out.'

Chance, realising talking was her way of coping with the fear, was happy to play along.

'The name change, all that stuff about channelling an Atlantean priestess, was it your idea?'

'Just part of Cornelius's act. He said most people were prepared to believe any old crazy shit you fed them, so long as you gave them the courtesy of putting on a good show. And, boy, did that son of a bitch know how to do a show. Sometimes, I almost believed him myself.'

'So, your name's not Lilith?'

'No. It's Eva.' She laughed nervously. 'Bell's not your real name, is it?'

'No.'

'You going to tell me what it is?'

He hesitated. A show of trust now would work in his favour.

'Gary. Gary Chance.'

'I was beginning to think there was something suspect about you, Gary Chance. The way you were always watching me. I thought you were onto me.'

Chance looked behind them. Still nothing. Picked up his step.

'Tonight was going to be my last in that place. Then it was goodbye Australia and hello Fiji, white sand beaches and cocktails.'

'You can still do that, though you might have to forgo plans for that first-class plane ticket.'

They reached a strip of dense scrub, plunged through it, emerged onto a dirt road, the shape of Tremont's station wagon visible in the gloom a couple of hundred metres ahead.

The engine kicked into life as they approached, the headlights illuminating the stretch of dirt road in front of it. The driver's door opened. Tremont got out and stood by the car

'Who is your friend?'

Chance tensed, alerted by the forced casualness in Tremont's voice, his lack of surprise at Eva's presence.

'Introductions later.' Chance tightened his grip on the spanner. 'We need to make tracks.'

'Sorry mate.' Tremont flashed a weak smile, lifted two palms towards Chance. 'The plan's changed.'

Swain emerged from the undergrowth at the side of the road, stood next to Tremont. He pointed a pistol, the barrel moving between Chance and Eva.

'Put the bag and the spanner on the ground and stand back.'

Chance dropped the bag on the ground and let go of the spanner. He tried to estimate whether he could reach Swain before the man could pull the trigger.

'Don't even think about it,' said Swain, reading his mind. 'Tough looking man like you, I figured you spilt your guts too quickly. So, when Dobbs and I found nothing at the front gate, I wasn't surprised.' Swain switched his gaze to Eva. 'But it was when I got back at the drying shed, found Cornelius bled out and no sign of either of you, that's when the alarm bells really went off. Tell me. Which of you did the boss?'

Eva smiled.

'Not that I care, but I always told Cornelius he shouldn't trust you. Pity he was too busy trying to get down your pants to listen.'

'You jealous, Joe?'

'You're not my type.'

'What, not Aryan enough?'

'Enough bullshit.' Swain gestured at Tremont with the barrel of his pistol. 'Check the bag.'

Tremont came forward, knelt, and unzipped the bag. His eyes widened at the sight of the money.

'Bring it here,' said Swain.

Swain took the bag in one hand, couldn't help himself, peered inside. Chance seized the opportunity, launched himself rugby tackle-style around Swain's stomach. It felt like hitting a brick wall. Swain grunted as the air was knocked from him. The gun skidded into a gully at the side of the road and the bag dropped to the ground. Bills spilled out, quickly picked up by the wind.

'Don't just stand there,' grunted Chance as he wrestled with Swain on the ground. 'Get the bloody gun.'

Tremont and Eva glanced at each other, had the same thought. Tremont moved first. Eva tripped him up as he grabbed the bag, kicked him in the side of the head. More bills escaped the bag as he hit the dirt.

Chance and Swain were off the ground, circling each other, both looking for a weakness to attack.

On the edge of his vision, Chance saw Eva reach into the side of her cowboy boot, withdraw something, and throw it. Swain howled as the knife she'd used on Cornelius bit deep into his shoulder. He lurched towards the shadows at the side of the road.

Chance stood stunned for a moment. Tremont lay groaning on the ground. Chance thought about helping his former partner, dismissed the idea as Swain re-emerged from the darkness, the pistol in his hand. He swayed like a drunk, his face set hard against the pain, aimed unsteadily at Chance, fired.

The shot went over his head and into the bushes behind him.

Chance made a desultory attempt to grab at some of the loose bills blowing in the air.

'Forget the money,' shouted Eva from the driver's seat of the car. 'Get in.'

Swain fired again. A spider web crack appeared in the rear passenger window.

Chance dived into the back seat. Eva slammed down on the accelerator. Several more shots sounded in the darkness behind them.

'Where'd you learn to use a knife like that?'

'Let's just say I had a misspent youth.'

'Lucky for me.'

'That's the second time I've saved your arse tonight,' she said.

'How will I ever repay you?' said Chance, stretching out on the back seat.

She smiled at him in the rear-view mirror. 'We'll figure out something.'

GREAT BOOKIE ROBBERY

ONE

Chance descended the stairs at the front of Flinders Street station, dodging the peak hour exodus of office workers rushing towards him to catch trains home.

As always, the fabric of the city felt different after his time away. He passed another large hole in the ground, felt a momentary pang of anxiety when he couldn't remember what had once stood there. More construction, more unfamiliar buildings, the low-rise central business district of his youth fading fast, replaced with a mass of towering glass and steel.

He paused to get his bearings and caught sight of Vera Leigh's bodyguard, Angel, looming over the passing foot traffic ahead of him.

Angel's red hair was pulled back in a tight ponytail, his eyes shaded by ever-present Ray Bans. He scanned the street, Terminator like. As he locked on Chance, Angel inclined his head and said something to a smaller man next to him. Loomis.

'Angel.' If he had another name, Chance didn't know it.

'Chance.'

'Hail fellow well met,' said Loomis.

'Loomis.'

'Vera told me you'd had some work done on your face. Was it with a hammer?' Loomis smiled at his own humour.

Loomis was somewhere in his sixties, if Chance had to guess, with a shoulder-length mane of snow coloured hair. Chance had spied him previously at one or two of Leigh's famous parties, but had never met him in person. Loomis had always stood at the edge of the crowd or sat in a far corner, and people came to him.

Loomis had large possum-like eyes and his nose and cheeks were criss-crossed with tiny red veins, a road map to years of excessive living. He wore a white business shirt, crumpled black suit, and scuffed black shoes, a bright blue paisley cravat and a confident smirk, the only give-aways there might be more to him than first appeared.

'Well, what are you waiting for, a gold embossed invitation?' Loomis's voice was a mixture of velvet and gravel. He emitted a wet cough, nodded towards the entrance to a building, stairs leading into the darkness. 'She's waiting for you down there.'

Chance realised they were standing directly outside one of the last adult cinemas left in the CBD. A big-breasted blonde in a yellow bikini peered down at them from a faded Perspex sign fixed to the front promising 'XXX fun'. The name of the establishment hung from an awning across the footpath, surrounded by flashing yellow lights, several of which no longer worked. A smartly dressed young woman, mobile phone to her ear, shot them a disapproving look as she hurried past.

Chance shrugged, made to go down the stairs leading from the footpath, felt a hand on his shoulder.

Angel stared at him from behind the shades. 'You know the drill.'

Chance raised both hands slightly. 'I don't think he likes me,' he said as Angel patted him down.

Loomis looked at Angel like he was a wild dog he was considering letting off the leash. 'He doesn't like anyone.'

Chance went down the stairs. He felt silly, realising how glad he was Eva wasn't with him.

The two of them had stolen another car in Byron, driven south together, constantly checking the radio for news about the botched cult job. There was nothing.

They took turns driving, the conversation guarded. Eva gave

him bits and pieces about her early life, a father dead before his time, her brief stint working in real estate. He reciprocated with select stories from his own life, nothing too deep or incriminating.

They stopped towards dusk at a town called Eden. Chance called Loomis, then tried to reconnoitre his way to an emergency stash of money he'd buried years ago. But the location—an abandoned weatherboard house—was gone, replaced by a long line of identical brick dwellings.

'Let me guess,' Eva said, as the two stood outside the house, 'just another temporary pause in your rocket ship-like ascent to criminal fame.' She smiled as she got out of the car, angled a hip at him. 'Maybe you can knock on the door, ask the new owner if they found your cash?'

They'd slept together that night. What started as an awkward mutual fumbling was soon the fierce slapping of their bodies against each other, as they fucked the last whisps of the previous night's adrenaline out of their systems. Chance fell asleep to the waves of light thrown through the cheap motel curtains by passing semi-trailers.

The next morning over breakfast Eva quipped it was only sympathy sex.

Chance laughed. 'Longest sympathy sex I've ever had.'

'Come off it, sunshine, don't think I didn't notice you eye fucking me all that time you were in the New Atlantis compound.'

'Guilty.' Chance put his hands up in mock surrender.

She flashed a sassy smile, her hair still wet and spiky from the shower, before shovelling a forkful of egg into her mouth. 'What next?' she said, through the food.

'I don't know about you, but I'm heading to Melbourne.'

'That call you made. Whoever it was, they offer you another job?'

Chance sipped his coffee, grimaced at how weak it was. 'Something like that.'

'I'm coming with you.'

Chance opened his mouth to protest, but she cut him off.

'Don't get me wrong, Gary. Killing Cornelius was as much to protect me as anything.' She picked up a crisp rasher of bacon, bit into it, her green eyes fixed on a point somewhere over his shoulder. 'I would've been the next suspect once he'd finished with you.'

She shrugged. 'Way I figure it, you owe me. Least you can do is let me tag along, recoup some of my losses.'

And it was done.

At the bottom of the stairs, a young man sat in a ticket booth reading a textbook. Chance slid the ten-dollar entrance fee through the half circle cut in the bottom of a greasy pane of glass.

Without looking up, the young man took the money, slid a ticket across the Laminex counter towards him. 'This is good until we close at four am.'

As Chance opened the door, a man in a business suit pushed past him on the way out, zipping up his fly as he walked. Chance stepped into a large, dark, low-ceilinged room containing several dozen rows of red vinyl seats, an aisle down the side leading to a door with a red exit sign, a strip of lights guiding the way. The room stank of body odour and air freshener.

On the screen, a heavily tattooed brunette was giving a blowjob to a preppy-looking guy sitting on a black leather couch wearing nothing but a baseball cap. The sound of her slurping and his half-hearted encouragement was broadcast from speakers mounted in every corner of the room.

Chance recognised Leigh from her customary turban. 'I haven't changed my look since the seventies,' she always said. She sat in the middle of the fifth row, one of only two patrons, the other an elderly man, his eyes glued to the screen.

'The prodigal son returns,' purred Leigh as Chance slid into the seat next to her. Without taking her eyes from the screen, she placed a spidery hand gently on his forearm. 'It's good to see you, Gary.'

Chance found the intimate gesture strangely out of character.
'I didn't know you were a film buff, Vera.'

'This?' She screwed up her nose. 'Sexy as wet shit, isn't it?'

'That's one way of putting it.'

'I'm sorry for what happened in northern New South Wales.'
She cast a quick sideways glance at him as she spoke. 'You can't
trust anyone these days.'

'It appears not.'

'I hear you made a friend though, so not a complete loss.'

Leigh's way of letting him know she had eyes everywhere.

'And you look good, dear, healthy and mean. That job the
Thai plastic surgeon did on your face makes you look deliciously
cruel. Honestly, it gives me goosebumps every time, especially in
this light.'

Leigh was referring to the wash up of another failed job. An
enforced exile in Thailand, a botched plastic surgery job that had
taken away his everyman features, replaced them with a face best
described as like an identikit picture in a tabloid newspaper.

On the screen, the man was now pumping mechanically away
at the woman from behind, the two of them expending as much
effort trying to balance themselves on the slim couch as fucking.

Chance shifted in his seat, averted his eyes to the ceiling and
listened to the sound of the man slapping the brunette's rump,
like he was riding a horse, her profanity-laden encouragement,
as he waited for Leigh to get to the point of the meeting.

'You know, the place wasn't always like this.' She moved her
hand from his forearm, languidly drew it across the air in front
of her. 'I used to strip here when I first arrived in Melbourne
from Sydney. It was a class joint then. Not the hole it is now.'

She exhaled loudly, slumped in her seat.

'The whole city has changed.' She reached into a leather
shoulder bag sitting on her knees, withdrew a silver flask. 'It's a
different place now.'

She unscrewed the cap, took a generous swig, offered it to
Chance.

He shook his head. It was unusual for Vera to mix drinking with business. 'Loomis said something about a job.'

'Always straight to the point, one of the things I like about you. I won't sugarcoat it. I'm in trouble, Gary. My club, the bastards are trying to force me out.'

The club, her S&M dungeon, was located on one of the last seedy streets of Melbourne's CBD, along with several nightclubs and a selection of down-market eateries. It didn't appear in any of city best of guides. She advertised strictly through word of mouth.

'Who's trying to force you out?'

'A real estate company, big money behind them, based in fucking Dubai, of all places. They've bought out nearly everyone else on the strip, want to demolish the lot and turn it in to shitty apartments, as if Melbourne doesn't have enough of them already.

'I have a long-term lease but they're finding all kinds of ways to squeeze and it's starting to hurt. They keep this up, it won't be long until I'm out on my arse.'

'Why not sell up and get out? They must be offering you a good price.'

'It's the principle of the thing, dear,' she swivelled to face him. 'Do you know how hard I've had to work to get to where I am now? I'll be fucked if I'm going to let a bunch of cashed up yuppies half my age and their foreign friends push me out before I'm ready to retire.'

Leigh took another swig from the flask.

'Besides, a lot of strange shit is happening. Sometimes I feel like I'm being followed. It's not just the business they want, it's like they're out to get me. I'm scared, Gary.'

Chance said nothing, watched the duo on the screen awkwardly change position, the woman straddling the man, groaning as she ground down on him.

The botched job in Byron Bay, placing Chance with someone as unreliable as Tremont, was the kind of mistake Leigh would never have made a few years ago. Add to that the daytime drinking, maybe the old girl was losing her touch.

Then again, it was not like her to panic for nothing.

Vera Leigh was the rarest of creatures, a working girl who had saved the money she'd made on her back and stayed in the game on her own terms. He'd heard the stories about how she'd risen through the ranks of Sydney's Kings Cross sex industry in the late 1960s, re-established herself in Melbourne in the seventies. She'd always been careful, acted through cut-outs like Loomis for the illegal stuff, paid what she owed on time.

Not only was her club one of the last of its kind in the city, but she was one of the few remaining links to an older Melbourne and its underworld. A crime scene that had comprised much more than drugs and the men and women who paid and protected the people who dealt with them.

Chance had worked for Leigh in the past as a bouncer and driver. He'd also done security at some of the private parties she'd thrown in her five storey apartment building on an anonymous dead-end alley in the heart of the Melbourne CBD.

He respected her the same way he respected any long-term survivor of the life. He was even prepared to admit to himself he liked her, her debauched sense of humour, and intolerance for bullshit. But he didn't trust her. Not one bit. And the glimpse of vulnerability she'd allowed made him uncomfortable.

'Let me cut to the chase, Gary.' A hardness crept into her voice. 'I need money and I need it fast or I'm done for.'

'If you're looking for a loan, Vera, I'm not exactly flush these days.'

'No. I have a job. It's lucrative, and I need someone I can trust. I'm even prepared to forgo the usual arrangements and offer you an even split.'

'Jesus, you must be desperate.'

'Don't be unpleasant, dear,' she said, exaggerated hurt in her voice. 'But, yes, I am.'

'What are we talking about?'

'Let's just say I am confident it will suit your particular skills.'

The couple on the screen moved into position as the man panted, clearly about to come. About time, thought Chance, averting his eyes. The entire cinema filled with an almost animal like roar as the actor ejaculated.

'That's not good enough,' said Chance as the screen went blank. 'I've had it with only getting part of the bloody story.' He made to get up. 'You want me to work for you, tell me everything, or you find someone else.'

'Okay, okay, Gary.' Leigh placed a hand on his arm, pulled him back into the seat.

A young professional looking couple walked down the aisle and sat a couple of rows in front of them, giggling at their own daring.

'It's a heist,' she whispered.

'Go on.'

'There's one catch.'

'Which is?'

'It already happened. Nearly fifty years ago.'

TWO

The back exit of the porn theatre opened onto a rubbish strewn bluestone lane; its walls covered in a bewildering swirl of graffiti. Angel sat in a car, engine idling, his bulk barely contained within the enclosed space.

The bodyguard edged the car into Melbourne's early evening traffic. The city appeared even more alien to Chance at night. Gleaming apartment buildings he couldn't remember from his last visit shot out of the ground at regular intervals along the journey.

Leigh sat next to him in the back of the vehicle. 'You still smoke rollies, Gary?'

'Yes.'

'Roll me one, would you dear?'

She let Chance light her cigarette, leaned back, closed her eyes and drew hard. 'That hits the spot,' she said, exhaling. 'My doctor tells me at my age I shouldn't be smoking. But, well, doctors, fuck 'em.'

Her lean figure and flamboyant personality had always made it easy to forget she was well into her seventies. But Chance saw the two years or so since he'd seen her had not been kind. Her face was gaunt, black rings beneath her eyes. The decline was more than physical. The way she slumped. Gone was her usual sprightliness, her movements deliberate and slow.

* * *

31

The duty station in the oncology ward was unattended. Most of the rooms off the carpeted passageway were silent and dark, but low light issued from the occasional chamber to reveal a motionless figure in bed, a relative or loved one sometimes at their side.

It was not Chance's first time on a cancer ward. He remembered his mother, diagnosed Boxing Day, her body already riddled with the illness, dead a month later. He could still remember the shock, how it broke something in him he didn't have the words to describe. He still didn't. His unanswered question then and now: was she as surprised as everyone else, or had she known all the time and kept it hidden? He didn't want to go where his thoughts were taking him, pushed them away as he trailed a few steps behind Leigh.

Leigh stopped at the entrance to one of the rooms and took a moment to compose herself before striding in, arms outstretched. She embraced a woman who rose from a chair next to a bed in which lay another, much older woman. A large window behind them revealed an expanse of brightly lit buildings and roads.

The bedridden woman was a husk, wispy grey hair splayed on the pillow, eyes closed, skin stretched. Condensation on the clear plastic of her breathing apparatus was the only sign of life.

After a hushed exchange, Leigh turned to Chance, who'd lingered in the doorway and motioned him to enter.

Leigh turned to the woman standing next to her, placed a hand on her shoulder. 'Sylvia, this is Mister Egan, the man I told you about.'

Egan was a false name associated with a past job. Chance wasn't clear why Leigh used it, but played along.

'Nice to meet you Mister Egan.' She said it in such a way Chance couldn't tell if she was in on the deception or not.

Sylvia Mundy was a middle-aged woman with lank, shoulder-length brown hair, a pinched face, brown eyes hooded by the exhaustion of her bedside vigil. Loose clothes hid any contours of her body. A woman folded in on herself.

'How's your mum?' said Leigh.

'Not great.'

'Well, at least she is being looked after.'

'Thanks to you, Vera. Seriously, without your financial help, I don't know what I would've—'

'Don't mention it, dear.' Leigh cut her off. 'It is the least I can do for Ruth.'

'The oncologist is recommending a second lot of chemo, but I'm not sure she's strong enough. It might be time to start thinking about palliative care options.'

'She's a tough old bird. She might surprise you.'

'Maybe. I'm starting to think the best thing might be to let the cancer take its course.'

'I am sure the doctors have her best interests at heart.'

Sylvia exhaled a short breath. 'Do you know why they put screws in the coffins of cancer victims?'

Vera shook her head.

'It's the only way to keep the oncologists from giving them more treatment.'

Sylvia led them to the table furthest from the other customers in the hospital café. While Leigh went to get coffees, she turned to Chance.

'What do you know about the Great Bookie Robbery?'

Local criminal lore. Australia's largest unsolved heist. Melbourne, April 1976: six masked gunmen stormed the Victorian Jockey Club on Queens Street in the city. The room was full of bookmakers settling after big race meets over the Easter weekend. A precision job with no casualties. At least until after the robbery.

'I know they never found out how much was taken,' said Chance.

'How much can you stuff into a hundred and eighteen pillow sized calico bags? Some say six million. But there were reports the take was as large as fifteen, maybe sixteen million, a bloody fortune thirty years ago. All we know is it was a hell of a lot more than the over one million reported to the police and the tax department as having been stolen.'

Sylvia paused to let her words sink in before continuing what was obviously a well-rehearsed spiel.

'The execution was flawless. The robbers rented a fourth-floor office in the same building above the Club and used it as their HQ to plan the job. That meant they were familiar with the building's layout. There's even rumours they did a dress rehearsal of the robbery while the Club was empty one weekend. For ages, the cops worked on the assumption the bandits had escaped with the money in a stolen white van. But they'd simply hidden it in a safe in their rented office, walked out of the building and returned several weeks later to retrieve it.'

Sylvia mouthed 'thanks' to Leigh as she placed a cup in front of her.

'The cops had no idea what had happened. They were casting all over the place for clues, even thought it might be an overseas gang. They offered a reward for information but got nothing, even though a lot of people in Melbourne's underworld had an idea who the bandits were.'

'Proper criminals back then,' said Leigh, her eyes momentarily sparkling with arcane criminal knowledge. 'Men with a code and real dash. Not the drug addled no-hopers that make up the scene today.'

Chance had met the kind of criminals Leigh was referring to and knew there was nothing glamorous or honourable about them. Most had started out as the boys of damaged fathers still living in the shadow of the war, had done time on the streets or in brutal facilities for youth offenders in which they were beaten or worse. As a result, they had grown into hard men without empathy. Individuals who would fight their own reflections if they couldn't find anyone else, would fall out over a woman, drugs, or money as easily as ordinary people changed a light globe. As the events that followed the Great Bookie Robbery showed.

'It wasn't until years later the cops even had any idea of some of the people involved,' continued Sylvia. 'Raymond "Chuck" Bennett was the mastermind of the operation and others who were involved were probably Ian Carroll, Laurence Prendergast, Leslie and Brian Kane, and Norman Leung Lee.'

The tiredness had lifted from Sylvia's face as she spoke. She ripped the top off a packet of sugar, stirred it into her cup.

'As it turned out, the cops were the least of the gang's problems. Brian and Les were standover men who made a major part of their living frightening other criminals. They thought their reputation in Melbourne's underworld entitled them to a much bigger share of the take than everyone else. But Bennett, no pushover, turned them down.

'All hell broke loose. One of Bennett's mates gave Brian a beating, which left him missing part of an ear. Les, a psychopath who made Brian look like a wallflower, threatened Bennett's family. Bennett and two others struck first and took out Les. Word was, they shot him. Made his body disappear. It was the first of a long line of corpses associated with the robbery.'

'Bennett was gunned down outside a city courthouse in 1979. He'd been arrested on some bullshit charge and while the police were escorting him from a holding cell to the courtroom, a man disguised as a lawyer shot him. Some say he was killed on the say-so of Brian Kane. Bent cops were suspected of facilitating the hit. No one was ever charged.

'It was Brian's turn next, shot in a crowded barroom in 1982, possible payback for the Bennett hit. They shot Carroll in 1983. Prendergast went missing in 1985, presumed dead. The only man ever charged in connection to the Great Bookie Robbery was Lee, nabbed spending new bank notes that had only just been delivered to the Jockey Club. But they couldn't find enough evidence to link him to the robbery, so he was acquitted. He never told them a thing. Lee was killed by cops in a botched robbery at Melbourne Airport in 1992.'

Chance glanced at Leigh. She was trying for impassive, like

the chaperone who didn't want to interfere, but couldn't keep the gleam of anticipation from her eyes.

'According to the newspapers, the last man linked to the robbery died in late 2017, a particularly unpleasant individual by the name Brian Grove,' said Sylvia. 'He was alleged to have helped launder part of the take from the heist.

'Officially, the case remains unsolved and the fate of the money unknown. There's been a lot of scuttlebutt and rumours. Some believe the money ended up in Manila, where Grove owned a bar. Others say it was quietly invested and the proceeds divvied up among the surviving relatives of the gang. It doesn't matter because I am interested in another part of the story: the twenty million in uncut South African diamonds taken by the gang but never reported.

'Oh,' Sylvia made an exaggerated show of raising her cup, paused it mid-air, 'do I have your attention now Mister Egan?'

'Keep going.'

'Bennett had known about the diamonds from an intermediary when he was planning the robbery, but had kept them secret from the Kane brothers. He didn't think Grove had the contacts to fence that kind of merchandise. Also, he didn't trust him and had to move fast before Les and Brian got wind the stones existed. So, he brought someone else in to handle that part of the job. Someone who had a more unique skill set than Grove. My father, George Mundy.'

Chance nodded for her to continue, his turn to act impassive.

'Dad agreed to help Bennett stash the diamonds until the heat was off, then launder them, either in Australia or overseas. But someone must have talked because word got out a couple of bent cops were going to lean on Dad for the diamonds and to give up the rest of the gang, kill him if he didn't come over. Then Brian Kane started hearing rumours and began asking around. Dad had to piss off out of the country. Fast.

'You know, even though I was only a child, I can remember the night he left. I was woken up by the sound of Mum crying, peeked from around the corner of my bedroom door and saw Dad, dressed in his favourite plaid sports jacket, madly tossing stuff into a suitcase. He had an expression on his face I'd never seen before—which I now realise was fear. He kissed mum before literally running out the door.'

Sylvia gave Chance a wan smile.

'That was June 10, 1976, less than a couple of months after the robbery. I was four years old. It was the last time Mum and I saw him.'

'What made your old man so special that Bennett approached him to launder the diamonds?'

She nodded, expecting the question.

'Let's just say Dad had certain abilities, and he knew a lot of people. That's all the detail you get for now until you agree to help,' she added, reading the look of scepticism on his face. 'I want you to help me locate my father, retrieve the diamonds, or whatever my father got for them. Vera tells me you're resourceful and can look after yourself and, Christ knows, with a face like yours, I wouldn't be surprised. What do you think?'

'That you've got to be fucking joking,' Chance said, louder than he meant to. A woman at a table near them looked up from her food, scowled in his direction. He leaned in, spoke in a hushed voice. 'You said you don't know where your father is. I'm not a private detective. How am I expected to find him?'

'No, I said, we hadn't seen him since he walked out of the house. But you're right. I don't know where he is.'

'And the bullshit story about diamonds, if it's even real, what on earth makes you think any money made from them hasn't long since disappeared? The robbery, what followed, was over forty years ago. For that matter, what makes you think your dad is even still alive?'

'The bastard's alive. I can feel it.'

Chance turned to Leigh. 'You believe this?'

'Point is, Mister Egan, I believe it,' replied Sylvia before Leigh could answer.

'Why?'

'Because of the men who watched our house for years after Dad disappeared, the cops who'd turn up at the front door to interview my mother at two in the morning, years after the Great Bookie Robbery took place. There's also the money that arrived in the mail for us, in envelopes without a return address, intermittently for the last four decades.'

'And you think those come from your dad?'

'Who else? Dad was born in 1940. That would make him seventy-eight. Not that old.'

'That's all you've got?'

'What else do you want?'

'How about some proof, real proof that he's still alive? You said so yourself, everyone associated with the job is dead—'

'But that's the bloody point. It was far too risky to even look for my father and the diamonds, while anyone else associated with the job was still breathing. Grove's death last year makes it a clean sweep. There's no one else left standing except Dad. Besides, I've managed to piece together other parts of the story. I'll give you all the information I have,' she paused, 'if you'll help us.'

Chance threw his head back, exhaled hard as he stared at the ceiling. 'Vera, I can't believe this is the job you dragged me back to Melbourne for.'

'Are you telling me you'd rather knock off another cult or some other bullshit score?'

'That was *your* bullshit score, Vera.'

Leigh dismissed his words with a flick of her spidery fingers, leaned close. 'Do you know how much twenty million in diamonds back then is worth today?'

'No.'

'At least ninety million dollars,' she said in a self-satisfied tone. 'And a third of whatever we recover is yours. Serious money.'

'If it exists, which I doubt.'

'Can you afford to take that risk? Because I can't,' Leigh shot back. 'I need this, dear boy, badly. If I don't get it, everything I've worked for is going down the toilet and I'm too old to start over.'

'And what about you, Miss Mundy? Why do you want to do this?'

She sat back, folded her arms in front of her.

'Mister Egan, or whatever your real name is, I am forty-seven years old. I've lived for most of my life in the same shitty brick veneer house my father walked out of forty-three years ago. The only exception were the three years I was with a useless excuse for a male who I married because he was the first man who looked at me twice. The rest of the time it was just the two of us, me and Mum, who spent her entire life expecting Dad to walk back through the front door and for everything to go back to the way it was.'

Her words came in short sharp thrusts, like a scalpel, cutting away dead flesh.

'Mum hasn't got much time—.'

Leigh started to speak, but Sylvia silenced her with an upheld hand.

'Please don't disagree with me, Vera. Mum will be dead soon and I'm getting old. I don't have any grand scheme. I want the fucking money.'

'He'll have spent it,' Chance said evenly. 'If he's still alive and the diamonds ever existed.'

'The envelopes we received in the mail say differently. My gut says differently. I'll give you all the information I have, but first you have to come in on the job. I don't tell you anything else until you're in.'

'And if by some miracle, I do find him, what do I do, just walk up to him and ask for the cash?'

'Dad destroyed two lives the night he walked out of our house. Mum's and mine because, stupidly, I felt so bad for her and spent most of my time since looking after her. And because, the truth be told, for a lot of those years I also fooled myself he was coming back, too. Once you find him, you do whatever you want. That's not part of the job I'm interested in. I want the money. Understood?'

The apple doesn't fall far from the tree, Chance thought, rising to his feet.

THREE

Hardigan waved at the nurse as she looked up from her paper-work.

She gave him a quick up and down, her face softening with recognition.

'Traffic bad again, Mister Teal.'

Hardigan smiled, searched his memory for her name. She had a strong, competent looking face, with a smattering of freckles, black hair pulled back in a tight bun.

'Absolutely terrible, Susan.'

She nodded, humouring his unspoken sentiment, not like it was in my day, how did the world ever get in such a state.

He'd used the same tone of affable disbelief the first time he'd visited Ruth Mundy, posing as an elderly friend, slightly flustered after the drive into town from the country. I know visiting hours are over, dear, it was the earliest I could get away after minding the grandkids, I won't stay long, something along those lines. The nurse had briefly weighed up the correct procedure against denying a terminal patient a visitor, waved him through.

Now the medical staff hardly gave him a second glance, an old man visiting a dying friend. Tall, in good condition for a guy his age, with a layer of fine straw-coloured hair. His only disconcerting feature were his eyes. Hard slivers of blue which bored right into you if got caught up in his gaze for too long.

As he walked down the dimly lit corridor, his chest tightened, breathing became harder. Hardigan reached out, steadied himself against the wall. Over a half a century later and a dark room, a confined space, a bad memory, any of them might set off his post-traumatic stress disorder. Of course, he only discovered that's what it was called years after he'd returned to Australia and the term still sounded unfamiliar whenever he said it aloud. He could be walking up a narrow set of stairs and he was suddenly back in the steaming jungle, feeling the heat and fear, hearing snatches of Vietnamese and Montagnard, mixed with cursing in a range of English tones.

He willed his body to push through it lest he draw attention to himself. Just like in the war, he told himself, nothing for it but to launch yourself headfirst into the narrow mouth of the tunnel. And when you reached the ninety-degree turn, keep crawling, a silenced Browning in one hand, the battery-powered lamp attached to your cap the only thing between you and complete all enveloping darkness.

When his breathing had steadied, Hardigan righted himself, continued walking until he reached Ruth Mundy's room. One pass by the door to reconnoitre the situation and see if it was safe to go inside.

A bedside lamp illuminated the motionless old woman, her daughter asleep in a chair beside her.

He walked across the carpeted floor without a sound, stood next to the dying woman. The Americans had moved through the jungle, smoking cigars, transistor radios blaring, almost like they wanted to attract the enemy's attention so they could unleash their superior firepower. It rarely worked out as they planned. The Australians and the South Vietnamese had used stealth, tried to surprise their enemies. The experience wasn't wasted on him.

Her fine grey hair, sprayed in a semi-circle around her head, reminded him of Kieu, her shoulder length hair the colour of tar. Kieu meant 'to be pretty' in Vietnamese and to a gangly young man fresh out of a small rural Australian town, she was the prettiest thing he had even seen. He whispered her name, still felt the same sense of wonder at the sound it made as he had when he first heard it in the Tu Do Street café back in Saigon.

Hardigan put his hand out to stroke the old woman's hair, his strong fingers calloused from working on the farm. He stopped himself, closed his eyes, jammed both hands deep into the pockets of his windbreaker. Sometimes the worst thing about being old was the feeling you were nothing more than decaying skin wrapped tight around too many sad memories.

When he opened his eyes, Ruth Mundy hadn't moved. Not much life left in the old girl. He could snap her neck like a twig, be doing her a favour. His eyes narrowed in recrimination at the daughter. You should just end it quickly, like he had with Kieu before the full force of her dementia had set in. They'd agreed on what to do and a mate, a former Australian army medic in Vietnam, had advised him what to use. Helium, deadly if enough of it is inhaled because it caused loss of consciousness due to oxygen deprivation, but a quick peaceful way to end it. He didn't need any bloody doctor to give him permission.

His mind snapped back to the reason he was here. It had started with that article in the newspaper, one of those colour pieces the journalists did whenever a famous criminal from the bad old days passed, taking their secrets to the grave.

The death of that fat shit Brian Grove hadn't interested Hardigan. But a couple of quotes from a former colleague still on the police force about Grove's little-known associate, George Mundy, a man rumoured to be involved on the fringes of the Great Bookie Robbery, piqued his curiosity. Hardigan wasn't aware of any sighting of Mundy since he'd pissed off out of the country in 1976.

The daughter, Sylvia, still living in the same house in Melbourne's northern suburbs, was easy to find. On a hunch Hardigan started following her, discovered Mundy's wife was dying of cancer in a Melbourne hospital. He staked her out, several weeks of nothing until he recognised one of the dying woman's visitors, a face from the past, a brothel madam called

Vera Leigh. Something was coming together; he felt it.

He'd had the same feeling earlier that evening, as he'd watched Leigh engage in a lengthy discussion with the daughter and a man with a face like five miles of unpaved road. The sense of lines connecting in ways Hardigan couldn't yet fathom but leading somewhere promising.

Everyone needed a hobby in retirement. Hardigan's had been waiting. He was good at it, and he sensed it was about to pay off. As his old man would've said, time to stir the possum.

FOUR

Chance was already regretting his decision to accompany Leigh back to her apartment complex in Melbourne's CBD.

'One drink to celebrate our new venture,' she said as they left the hospital.

'I haven't said I'd do the job, Vera.'

She ignored him, took a sip from her silver hip flask.

He'd agreed to come because the conversation might yield useful information and he was always in the market for that. But the last thing he wanted was to spend the night drinking with the morose old woman, whose grip on reality Chance was starting to wonder about.

As the service elevator creaked to a stop on the fifth and top floor of Leigh's place, she dropped her shoulder bag on to the floor and made a direct line for the well-stocked bar cart parked next to a press studded leather couch that dominated the room.

Chance stepped out of the elevator. The room was familiar to him from the times he'd worked security for one of Leigh's parties. Leigh had seldom mingled with her guests. 'That bunch of piranhas, you've got to be kidding,' she'd once quipped. She preferred to watch the action on the bank of screens connected to closed-circuit cameras rigged throughout the sprawling apartment complex. Reclining on the leather couch, she'd glance at the screens, exchanging small talk with Chance. Rumour had it more than the occasional guest had received a videotape in a plain brown envelope with a note threatening to expose his or her nocturnal activities unless money was paid or a certain course of action abandoned.

The screens were dead now. Chance wondered if the closed-circuit television system still functioned at all or, like Leigh and her surroundings, had fallen into a state of disrepair. Various pieces of mismatched furniture, some of it antique, others seemingly rescued from second-hand office sales, were arrayed around the room in no discernible pattern. On one table sat at least a dozen old analogue phones. The pièce de résistance was in a far corner next to the door to Leigh's bedroom, a diorama featuring several stuffed foxes, their fur in tatters.

She dropped cubes of ice into a cut glass tumbler, selected one of a dozen bottles arrayed on the cart and poured a generous measure of clear liquid. She drank, holding the glass in both hands.

'What's your poison?' she said, placing her glass on a heavy wooden coffee table. An inlay of chessboard squares peeked out from under piles of old porno magazines and newspapers.

'Whisky, neat.'

She handed the drink to him. He sipped. Single malt, not the watered-down stuff she normally served to guests.

Leigh sat on the couch, pulled at her turban. It unravelled to reveal straight shoulder length hair, once raven black now almost completely grey. She took another hit of her drink. They exchanged generalities about their few mutual acquaintances.

Not wanting to prolong the occasion by getting comfortable, Chance moved around the room taking in the framed photographs that peppered the walls. Some were in colour, others black and white. They all showed Leigh posing at various social events and in exotic foreign locales with well-dressed, well-fed, mainly male companions.

'You've certainly led an interesting life, Vera.'

'No need to talk about me in the past tense,' she snapped. 'I'm not in the ground yet. I've certainly got enough fight left in me to take on the bastards trying to close me down.'

Chance said nothing.

'Especially with your help,' she added.

He ignored the comment. He was trying to think of something to say that wasn't about the diamonds and Leigh's financial woes, when one of the images on the wall caught his attention. A simple wooden frame containing a pencil sketch of a double-storey Victorian era building in the middle of a field. Two large brick buildings connected by a middle section, a series of rooms running along an enclosed wooden veranda on both levels. The building on the right had an imposing arched entranceway.

He gently lifted it from the wall, blew away a layer of fine dust, held it up for Leigh to see.

'That's just something I did myself,' she said.

'I didn't know you sketched Vera,' Chance said, trying to inject a playful tone into his voice.

'My boy, what you know about me would comfortably fit on the back of a large postage stamp with space to spare.'

'Where is it?'

Leigh looked at the image. Her face softened with an expression Chance had never seen on her before. If he had had to describe it, he would have said regret.

'Where I left my heart.' She drained her glass. 'Amongst other things.'

Chance waited for her to say more. Instead, she half-closed her eyes and held out her empty glass. 'Be a love, Gary, fetch me another.' Her words were slightly slurred, tiredness and the drink getting the better of her.

'So will you do this job for me?' she murmured as she accepted the drink.

'I'm prepared to meet Sylvia here tomorrow, as agreed, and hear the rest of what she has to say. That's the best you'll get tonight. And fair warning, I'll be bringing a friend.'

Leigh shrugged. 'You drive a hard bargain.'

'I learnt from experts,' said Chance affectionately.

* * *

'Christ, Gary, you sound like you actually believe her?'

'I'm not sure "believe" is the right word. Let's say I've got an open mind to the possibility what Vera and the Mundy woman are saying might be true.'

After leaving Leigh's place, Chance texted Eva to meet up with him in the city. He didn't feel like going back to the serviced apartment in the Docklands they were staying in, an off-the-book's arrangement through one of Eva's real estate mates. Like the name suggested, Docklands was an old port complex that had gone under the wrecking ball to be replaced with a sprawling stretch of high-rise apartments and shops, populated, as far as Chance could tell, mainly by overseas students and an army of short stay Airbnb renters. It was a ghost town after dark. Chance half expected to see tumble weeds blowing down the streets.

Chance told Eva the details of the hospital conversation over dinner. She didn't say much while he spoke, only asked for the occasional clarification.

After the meal they went walking along the promenade lining the Yarra River. It was crowded with people making the most of the late summer evening. They filled the long stretch of restaurants and bars that fed into the huge casino complex, built in the 1990s.

Chance leaned against the railing and rolled a cigarette as he watched the lights from the buildings behind him reflected on the Yarra's surface. The night hid a multitude of sins, including the shit brown colour of the water.

'Your share, half my cut, could be as much as twenty million. That's a lot of trips to Fiji.'

'Maybe.' She leaned next to him. 'What would you do with yours?'

'Not sure.'

'You're not sure about a lot of things.'

'I'm sure I've had enough of this life.'

'You sound like my father. He said he always wanted to get out of the life.'

'Sounds like a smart man.'

'Was. He's long gone. And, no, he wasn't smart. He was an average musician and an even worse criminal, who never saw the inside of the jail cell he didn't like. He died in one of those cells with no more ambition than to get a bit of prison homebrew and smoke a few jailhouse durries. The only useful things Liam McCulloch ever did for me was to help me know my way around cars and teach me how to use a knife. "Evelyn, a girl has got to be able to protect herself," he used to say. And he would know.'

'You dislike what your father was so much, how come you're following in his footsteps? And with a man just like him?'

'You're not like him, far as I can tell.' She moved close so their shoulders were touching. 'Wouldn't be here if I thought you were.'

She ran a hand through her thick hair, looked straight ahead.

'And as for following in his footsteps, I don't intend to die penniless in a Perth jail cell, if that's what you mean.'

Chance turned around, leaned against the railing, exhaled cigarette smoke as he watched the crowd that was thinning as the night wore on: young couples still in their office clothes, large family groups of tourists from Asia, India and the Middle East. He noted the occasional glance in his direction, never held for too long. Check out Mister Identikit face and the attractive older lady.

'I'll tell you something else Dad used to say. "If it smells like a pig, looks like a pig, and makes a noise like a pig, it's probably a pig".'

'Maybe.'

She glared at him in a way that made it clear, "maybe" wasn't going to cut it.

'I'll grant you, the whole story is crazy, but what if it's true?'

'Does that mean you trust these women?'

'Hell no, not as far as I could comfortably spit out a brick.' Chance crushed the remains of his rollie with the heel of his boot. 'Sylvia Mundy is bitter and angry as hell and wants payback from her father. That's probably clouding her judgement.

'Vera's desperate for money, and desperate people don't always think straight. She's also—' Chance paused to search for the right words '—not as sharp as she used to be and drinking heavily. But despite all that, she's not stupid. She hasn't got where she is by chasing ghosts and taking unnecessary risks. She's still a tough businesswoman and if she thinks there's money to be made, she's probably right.'

The harsh city lights seeped through the flimsy curtains of their apartment. Chance lay in the semi-darkness, covered in the scent of Eva's body, her taste in his mouth, turning over the mechanics of the job in his head.

It was just after midnight. Eva hadn't said anything since rolling off him half an hour earlier, but he could feel her awake next to him.

'This might get real dangerous, real quick,' she whispered.

Chance smiled, knowing she was in.

'With this much money and this collection of people, I'd say almost definitely. Which is why I need you watching my back.'

'I suppose I can clear my schedule, give you a hand. But if this goes south, I'll be out, fast. You can bet on it.'

FIVE

A monosyllabic Angel patted Chance and Eva down, before escorting them into the service elevator that took them to the fifth floor. Angel stood by the door, ushered them into Leigh's inner sanctum.

The only difference from last night were the dust motes dancing in the pale light that crept between the crack in the heavy red velvet curtains. Chance took it all in again without comment but could tell Eva was working hard to mask her reaction.

Leigh sat on the same leather couch, clad in a black kaftan, leggings, and a lime green turban. Chance noted the empty glass tumbler in front of her. Not a good sign. The others sat in matching leather seats around the wooden coffee table.

Loomis was dressed in the same clothes as the previous night, had probably slept in them, if he'd slept at all. Daylight revealed the dirt around his collar and cuffs, hair greasy and wild, eyes rimmed by something Chance thought might be eye shadow. The old man acknowledged Chance with a nod, his attention fixed on the makings of a joint on the table in front of him.

Sylvia Mundy appeared younger than she had at the hospital. Her hair was pulled back in a tight ponytail, her face freshly scrubbed. Having a purpose other than caring for her sick mother obviously agreed with her.

Having agreed to let Chance do most of the talking, Eva

stood silently as he made the introductions. Leigh acknowledged her with a mix of curiosity and thinly veiled hostility. Chance leaned forward, mouthed the words, 'play nice'.

Loomis stood, made an exaggerated show of taking Eva's hand, kissing it. 'Welcome to our little gathering Miss McCullough.'

'So, are we to take it from your presence with us this morning that you are in on the job?' said Sylvia, pointedly ignoring Eva.

'We're here and keen to hear what else you've got to say,' said Chance.

Sylvia drew a deep breath, was about to protest when Leigh interjected.

'I think that will do just fine for starters, won't it, Sylvia dear?'

She nodded, her face becoming pinched.

'And, before you ask,' Chance addressed Leigh directly, 'Eva's share of anything we recover comes out of my end.'

Leigh acknowledged the statement with a slight wave of a hand.

'I've briefed Eva on last night's discussion at the hospital, so we can cut to it,' said Chance. 'You mentioned your dad had special skills that made him the right person to fence the diamonds.'

Sylvia took a deep breath.

'Dad was in the army, deployed to Vietnam. I don't know what he did exactly,' she emphasised the last word, 'but it was something to do with military intelligence.'

'He was a spy?'

'Something like that, yes.' She shrugged. 'Mum says he never really talked about it. Dad was already in the army when they met, and they'd only been married a couple of months before he was deployed. The few times she did broach the subject, he told her it was classified, and he couldn't speak about it.

'Compartmentalisation was certainly one of Dad's talents. Anyway, he was discharged in 1971, the year before the last Australian combat troops were withdrawn. I suppose Mum was just happy to have him back, so she didn't push him on it.'

Sylvia reached for a manila envelope on the table in front of her, withdrew a square photograph and handed it to Chance. 'This is the only image I have of him during the war, taken somewhere in South Vietnam.'

The photo showed a tall, fit looking man with crew cut hair, dressed in slacks and a short-sleeved white shirt, about to get into a jeep, washed out jungle foliage behind him. Aviator sunglasses covered his eyes, and he had a non-committal smile that betrayed nothing. His left hand was curled around the grip of a black attaché case. George Mundy as the spook from central casting. Chance turned the photo over. No inscription. He passed it to Eva.

'I did a bit of digging, looked in the archives of the National War Memorial in Canberra. True to his word, for once, his file is still classified.'

Eva cocked an eyebrow in Chance's direction. He ignored her, maintained his focus on Sylvia.

'I'm not entirely sure what Dad did after the war, but it was all illegal. Fencing stolen materials, the occasional armed robbery. I suspect there was more but can't prove anything. Again, Mum was never very forthcoming, assuming she even knew.'

'Surely you must've been able to find more than that?' Chance spoke more forcefully than he intended.

'Believe me, the lack of particulars is not for want of looking,' rasped Loomis. He struck a match and lit the joint.

'He's right,' said Sylvia. 'I've done a lot of digging. For a while I even had a private investigator on the case, generously paid for by Vera, but he didn't find out much more than I already knew.'

Chance glanced hard at Leigh. She dismissed this piece of information with a shrug.

Eva handed the photo back to Sylvia. 'Are you saying you've found no records for him at all?'

'Hardly a trace, Miss McCulloch, which is itself strange, wouldn't you say?' Loomis grinned, exhaled a lungful of sweet-smelling smoke.

'Someone who wanted to cover his tracks and was good at

Andrew Nette

'Almost like he was trained to do it, wouldn't you say?' said Loomis.

'Anyway, the little I have been able to gather is here.' Sylvia patted the manila envelope.

'Friends, acquaintances?'

'All those I know about are dead.'

'Natural and unnatural causes,' Loomis added mischievously.

'Not so much a low profile as the invisible man,' said Chance.

'The 1970s were a different time.' Tendrils of smoke dribbled from Loomis's nostrils. 'There was still the hint of possibility, not like this grey age of bureaucracy and computerised surveillance. Back then, old Gods and certainties were crumbling as the young sought to assert their place in the world. There was a sense of revolution in the air, the future was ours to be claimed.'

Loomis smiled at Chance and his companion like an elderly relative who'd had too much to drink at a family Christmas gathering and forgotten the point he was trying to make.

'At least what I can remember of it, I was out of it most of the time. My point is, amid the political convulsions, hollow men like George Mundy moved unseen and largely unrecorded, plying their dark trade.'

'Which was?' said Eva.

Loomis emitted a moist cough. 'Ah, well, that is the mystery we are all gathered here to solve.'

'Tell us more about what happened after the robbery,' said Chance. 'How did your dad get out of the country?'

'A berth organised through the Ships Painters, Painters and Dockers Union,' said Sylvia. 'Ray Bennett was a member.'

A union active on Melbourne's waterfront in the sixties and seventies, Chance recalled. Also, a front for sly groggers, gunmen, pimps, armed robbers and standover men.

'That got him to Manila, where from what the private investigator was able to piece together, he spent several months as a guest of Brian Grove.'

Sylvia paused, rummaged through the folder until she found another photo 'This was taken in Manila. Probably in the bar owned by Grove.'

Mundy in a tropical shirt, a stubby of beer in one hand, a small Asian woman in the other. The woman stared glassy eyed at the camera. She wore a skimpy bikini, a disk with a number pinned to her bra. Fairy lights, more people in the background, the gender split strictly Caucasian males and Asian women.

Slim faced, his hair longer than it had been in the army, Mundy stared directly into the camera with the rictus smile of someone who clearly hated having their photo taken but tried to hide it. Chance thought he detected a trace of menace in Mundy's eyes.

'From Manila he travelled to Bangkok before the trail went cold. Lots of rumours: that he went back to the Philippines where he was murdered; that he went to live in Hong Kong; that he was thrown out of a plane over a stretch of jungle in Thailand by persons unknown for refusing to divulge where the diamonds are. I don't believe any of them.'

'Why?'

'As I said last night, there was the money sent to Mum and me at semi-regular intervals.'

'How?'

'Plain envelopes left in our post box. Untraceable. There were also the cops who came around to interview mum.'

'Can you remember their names, anything about them?'

'Not much, they were cops. Always the same two men. Said they were making official inquiries related to the Bookie Robbery.' Sylvia bit her lip. 'One was tall, sandy haired. The other had a gut, balding. They talked like cops, you know, matter of fact but with a nasty undercurrent, like they could turn on you at any moment.

'I remember seeing the sandy haired man once or twice, sitting in his car outside our house, which was strange to say the least. Anyway, the two of them always came across like they knew far more than they were giving away. And whenever they talked to Mum, the conversation always came back to Dad's whereabouts, so I put two and two together.'

'And got what?'

'That they didn't really give a shit about solving the robbery case. They were trying to find the diamonds.'

'When was the last time they came around?'

'A long time ago, the early nineties.'

Chance sat back, folded his arms, made no effort to hide his frustration that what she was giving him was mostly dead ends.

'There is one last thing.' Sylvia gave Chance a wry smile. 'The private investigator wasn't completely useless.' She handed him a photocopy of a newspaper cutting.

Eva leaned in close next to Chance and peered at the page with him. It was an article from a newspaper called the *Philadelphia Inquirer*, dated January 1987. The top half was taken up by a grainy but reasonably clear photograph. It showed a man, swaddled in an overcoat, scarf and hat, a belligerent expression on his beefy face, emerging from a large convertible, grimy snow on the ground at his feet. Another man held the car door open for him. Other members of his entourage, maybe bodyguards, were visible in the background. According to the caption, the man getting out of the car was Salvatore Luchese, president of Local 30 of the Philadelphia Roofers Union.

Chance read the story. The forty-three-year-old Luchese was being tried for the slaying of his predecessor, Anthony 'Sonny' Rosata. Chance had to concentrate hard to make out the faded newsprint. Rosata's death was one of several murders alleged by the police to be connected with a wider turf war over drugs, illegal gambling and loan sharking taking place over a stretch of territory from southern Pennsylvania through to New Jersey and Atlantic City.

'What has this got to do with George Mundy?' said Chance, when he had finished reading.

'Look more closely at the picture,' said Eva.

Chance looked at the cutting again, noticed the man holding the door open for Luchese. Like the other men in the picture, he was swaddled against the cold, but his face, older but unmistakable. George Mundy.

'Luchese was a major figure in the Philadelphia mob scene,' said Sylvia, patting the folder. 'It's all here.'

'What was your father doing in Philadelphia in 1987?'

'That is the conundrum,' said Loomis through a cloud of marijuana smoke.

Chance took out his tobacco, started to roll a cigarette, his mind working through the possibilities.

Her eyes on Chance, Leigh sat forward on the couch, the pause in the conversation her cue to speak. 'Dear, how would you like to take a little trip to America?'

SIX

Tremont had been waiting at the pre-arranged spot to meet Chance on the edge of the New Atlantis compound, when a big man emerged from the undergrowth, pointed a gun at him and said: 'My name is Swain and I'm your new business partner.' Tremont, who didn't feel any major loyalty to Chance, was in no position to argue.

After Chance and the woman had driven off, Tremont only had time to grab a couple of wads of cash before the first cult members arrived. The sight of Cornelius's followers trying to catch loose bills amid the mounting storm reminded Tremont of those clips of Japanese game shows Celeste had showed him on YouTube, contestants grabbing money in a Perspex tube. Nothing like half a million in loose cash fluttering in the wind to make the average nutcase forget about the imminent arrival of Atlantean spirits and focus on more material matters.

Tremont crouched beside Swain as thick drops of rain started to fall. His head throbbed where the woman had kicked it, and he pondered making a run for it before the police arrived or the cult members discovered them.

But Swain's gaze was on him. He suggestively fingered the pistol tucked into the front of his jeans to emphasise the unspoken point. Tremont smiled weakly and reasoned his best chance of getting out of this situation was to stick with Swain. Even wounded, he looked like he could handle himself.

'Follow me,' Swain hissed as he disappeared into the darkness.

Tremont trailed the rapidly moving shadow in front of him, the rain heavy. Wet foliage slapped against his face. Once or twice, he thought Swain had left him behind before his hulking form reappeared, pausing to let him catch up.

The thick bush opened to a clearing, a squat shadow materialising into a white minivan as they drew closer. Tremont could make out the symbol of Cornelius's cult, a cross in concentric circles on the side.

Tremont drove while Swain pulled off his T-shirt, scrunched it into a ball, and held it against his shoulder to staunch the blood from his knife wound. He leaned back in the passenger seat, eyes closed.

'I'll have that bastard Chance under my boot and then deal with the bitch who stabbed me,' he said under his breath. 'But first I need to get this seen to.'

'There's a hospital not far away,' said Tremont.

'No,' Swain snapped. 'No fucking hospital. You got a place near here?'

'In Byron,' said Tremont meekly.

'Drive to it, we'll figure something out from there.'

Tremont snatched the occasional sideways glance at Swain's tattoos as he drove. A mass of swirling ink that looked almost like armour ran down one side of his muscular body. The word 'Valhalla' was clearly visible on his exposed breast, above what looked like three interlinked triangles.

Tremont wanted to know what had happened back in the cult compound but knew it wasn't the time to ask. He calmed himself by breathing deeply and flexing his hands open and shut on the steering wheel, a variation of a relaxation technique Celeste had taught him.

Celeste made it a habit of saying what she thought, when she thought it, as if there was no internal interlocutor between her brain and mouth. But even she was silent as Swain followed Tremont into the motel room and sat down hard on the couch, the blood-soaked T-shirt still clamped to his shoulder.

He leaned his head back against the couch and faced the ceiling. 'Have you got anything to fix my shoulder?' he said to no one in particular.

Swain watched, lizard like, as Tremont counted out the bank notes he'd managed to grab, while Celeste rummaged about in the bathroom.

'We're not going to get far with three thousand and change.' A wave of exhaustion swept over Tremont. He slumped in a chair opposite Swain, his clothes soaked, spied what was left of a gram of coke on a small makeup mirror amid various left-over joint fixings on the coffee table between them. Just what the doctor ordered. A quick line to take the edge off the night, help him think about what steps to take next.

He pulled the table towards him. As he started to push the white powder into a line with an old business card, Swain's booted foot kicked hard against the table. Tremont sat up in shock as the table fell onto its side.

'What the fuck,' wailed Tremont.

'You're not a degenerate drug dealer are you, Carl?'

'No.'

'Drugs are poison and dealers are the enemy of every decent white man. No more drugs.'

Tremont looked mournfully at the white powder sprinkled on the shag pile.

'If drugs are so bad, what were you doing working for Cornelius?' Tremont said, the retort helping him to recover a bit of lost pride.

'The ends justify the means.'

Celeste came back into the room to right the coffee table and disappeared again. She returned a few minutes later, placed a bowl of steaming water on the table, along with what she had managed to forage: Mercurochrome, a needle and thread, and a yellowed bandage that had seen better days.

Swain dropped the bloodied T-shirt on the floor as Celeste perched on the couch next to Swain.

'It's not deep but it'll still need a few stitches,' said Celeste.

'I was prepared to overlook Cornelius's degenerate ways, Carl, his stealth program of genocide against the white race, to get money for the resistance.'

'What resistance are you talking about? You some kind of Nazi?'

Swain winced slightly as Celeste dabbed Mercurochrome laced cotton on his wound. She paused. He nodded at her to continue.

'I'm not a Nazi, Carl, or some crazy doomsday prepper. I'm a racial realist.'

Tremont looked at him blankly.

'Which means I want to take action to save my race and for that, I need money. I don't have a problem with anyone who is a different race to me as long as they keep to themselves and their own country.'

'Sounds like a Nazi to me,' said Tremont, with more defiance than he felt.

Swain ignored the comment, locked eyes with the woman. 'You're doing well—'

'Celeste.'

'Thanks, Celeste.'

He lay back, head facing the ceiling.

'Talking about race, that olive skin of yours, I'm betting that's not from spending too much time on the sun bed.'

'Go on, tell him, Carlo.' Celeste giggled.

'Carlo.' Swain's mouth curved into an imitation smile. 'Sounds Italian to me.'

He was named Carlo Tremonti at birth. His parents, poor shit kickers from Calabria who came to Melbourne in the early 1960s, squeezed out three children, and spent their lives working in a nearby factory. Tremont had anglicised his name when he left home in his twenties in the hope it would avoid the racism he'd been mercilessly subjected to by his Anglo schoolmates.

'If it is any consolation to you, my grandfather fought with the Germans.'

Tremont felt a stab of self-loathing at his pathetic attempt to curry favour with Swain. He'd only even seen a grainy photograph of his grandfather, Lorenzo Tremonti. Taken at his wedding, it showed a thin man, with a dark complexion same as Carl's, in a cheap suit, smiling crookedly at the camera. Conscripted by Mussolini, dispatched to the Russian front and never heard from again.

'If that's the case, I might have to consider you an honorary white man.' Swain played with one of Celeste's red curls as she threaded a needle and held it up to him.

'This is going to hurt,' she said.

Swain nodded at her to continue.

'Now, Carl, tell me about the job with Chance,' he hissed through gritted teeth. 'Every single detail.'

Tremont told Swain everything as he watched Celeste stitch up the knife wound with a skill he didn't know she possessed.

Swain showed little sign of pain, only asked questions as Tremont talked, expressed particular interest in Chance's Melbourne contact, Loomis, the front man for a woman called Leigh. What did he know about them? Tremont recounted a party he'd attended at Leigh's place in Melbourne's CBD several years ago, where he'd been first introduced to Loomis.

'Do you reckon you'd be able to find that apartment again?'

Tremont had known his share of crazies. They came with the cult busting business. But none of them had scared him as much as the big man sitting across from him. He knew he was safe with Swain only so long as he was useful. And right now, his knowledge of Leigh's networks, slender as it was, was the only leverage he had.

'Yeah, sure.'

Celeste leaned in closer than she needed to as she finished the job off. One small backstitch and then she made a loop over the point of the needle, pulled the thread through the loop, cinching at the base the fabric, then cut it off.

Tremont's head throbbed. He realised it was hours since he had eaten.

'Celeste baby, could you fix something to eat.'

'I'm not your slave, Carl, get it yourself.' Her eyes were on Swain as she spoke. He smiled, reached out, slid his hand up her body until it rested on one of her thighs.

Tremont spent a mostly restless night on the couch, a pillow over his head to block out the sound of Swain and Celeste having sex in the bedroom, trying to figure out how things had gone so wrong so quickly.

He'd drifted off to sleep at some point, dreamed of the time he'd tended bar on a cruise liner. It was after his divorce and when his used car business had gone bust. A mate had suggested it, made it sound like a floating holiday, lots of free time and lots of bored women with nothing to do and twelves bars throughout the ship to do it in. As things turned out, there was minimal free time, and the customers were strictly off limits to the hired help.

But there'd been one passenger, a businessman who sat at the bar Tremont tended while his wife sunned herself topside, the kind of man who was always looking for someone to talk to. He told Tremont a story about his daughter being in a cult and how he'd had to outlay serious money to hire someone—a cult buster was what he'd called him—to get her out. The more the man talked, the more Tremont started thinking that was a hustle he might get into.

Tremont woke up to sex sounds. What he wouldn't give to be back on the boat, as far away from Swain, Celeste and the whole damn mess as possible.

Tremont felt something hard in his side. He looked up, groggy, a huge shadow looming over him. Swain came into focus, naked from the waist up, the tatts, the butt of the pistol protruding from over the belt of his jeans. His arm in some kind of makeshift sling, more proof of Celeste's newfound medical prowess.

Swain nudged him hard again with his booted foot. 'Check out time.'

Tremont sat up, the events of the previous evening coming into focus like a speeding truck. The room was dark, the bedroom door was closed, a crack of light along the bottom. He could hear Celeste moving about on the other side.

'Where are we going?'

'Melbourne.'

SEVEN

They ditched the New Atlantis minivan on the outskirts of Grafton, about two hundred kilometres south of Byron Bay, replaced it with a second-hand Toyota Hilux. Tremont and Celeste took turns driving while Swain sat in the back, his arm in the sling, keeping up a continuous patter of white nationalist bullshit. How the white race had to stand up to foreign invaders on our shores. What would happen to all the race traitors who worked for the state and invited them. And the fate of corporations who replaced hard working whites by employing those foreign invaders.

Tremont tried to ignore Swain, but Celeste hung on his every word. The apparent joy his former girlfriend took in shifting her sexual favours from him to Swain was one thing; her transformation from dope smoking, hippy chick, into right-wing race warrior was even more perplexing. And annoying.

Celeste, who had hardly worked a day in her life thanks to her Sydney software start-up owning father, whose generosity she had repaid by running away to the New Atlantis commune, was a different person. She and Tremont had been sitting in the Hilux in a parking lot outside a shopping complex in a town somewhere near the Victoria border, while Swain made some calls from a payphone, when a group of African youths passed in front of them. Tremont could have sworn he'd heard Celeste curse them under her breath.

They hit the outskirts of Melbourne three days after leaving

Byron, as dusk bathed the entire city in fiery orange. They spent the night in a motel near Melbourne Airport and the next morning, Swain made Tremont take him to Leigh's.

It has been several years since Tremont was last in Melbourne. That and the fact the entire central business district resembled a construction zone due to the expansion of the city's underground rail loop made Tremont nervous he might not be able to find the address.

He tried hard to hide his uncertainty as he ushered Swain up a street running along the Yarra River, passing several narrow bluestone lanes, one of which Tremont was sure contained the entrance to Leigh's multistorey apartment building. He doubled back a couple of times until he located what he was certain was the right one. He stopped within sight of a black painted metal door, taking care not to come into the field of view of a closed-circuit camera mounted above.

'It's that one.'

Swain said nothing, pressed himself into the entrance to a disused loading bay, surveyed the narrow five storey building.

'And she has all five storeys?' he said without taking his eyes off the building.

'She lives on the top floor, so yes.'

'Security guards?'

'How the hell do I know, man, I just went to a party here. I didn't even meet Leigh.'

Tremont's anger wilted as Swain turned his large head towards him, flexed his wounded shoulder menacingly, and returned his gaze back to the building.

'It might help if you could tell me what you're planning.'

'That's on a need-to-know basis, Carl, and right now you don't need to know. Do you remember the inside layout?'

Tremont considered how to best play the question.

'Enough, yeah.'

'Enough to direct us around if we can get inside?'

Tremont nodded confidently. Truth was he'd drunk his share

of vodka and imbibed generously from a tray of constantly replenished cocaine that floated around the proceedings, so his memories of the night weren't the sharpest. Most of the party had taken place in a large oak panelled space on the ground floor. This was connected to a large bar area and what he assumed was a kitchen. Guests who found the combination of drugs, drink and general debauchery conducive to more intimate activities were able to avail themselves of a number of much smaller rooms on the second storey.

At one point in the evening, Tremont and a woman he'd just had sex with broke off from what was showing all the signs of becoming a full-blown orgy and drunkenly explored the third and fourth stories of the building, an assortment of rooms of different sizes, crammed with a bewildering array of mismatched furniture. Some passageways ran between the rooms while others led inexplicably to dead ends. At least two sets of stairs wound their way through the building.

In their drunken state they had tried to go up to the fifth floor, where their mysterious host was rumoured to reside, but their way had been blocked by a large, muscular man, his eyes hidden by a pair of Ray-Bans. Tremont decided against volunteering any of this information for now in favour of drip feeding it slowly. He hoped that particular bouncer was still in Leigh's employ and would give Swain a run for his money.

After about twenty minutes Swain told Tremont to take him back to the motel to meet Celeste and get the car.

'Do you reckon you can direct us to the Flemington Race-course,' he said.

'Yeah, what's there?'

'A bit of extra assistance.'

Carl Tremont watched Celeste run a finger down the heel of an imitation samurai sword. Swain stood next her, dressed in a leather motorcycle jacket and dark sunglasses. His arm was out of the sling for the first time since he was stabbed, and Tremont noticed him continuously flexing his shoulder, testing the improved movement in his body.

Swain had directed Tremont to drive to an outdoor adventure exhibition in a hangar at the back of Flemington Racecourse. The vendors selling camping equipment were easily outnumbered by the number of stalls selling army surplus gear and various types of what Tremont suspected was semi-legal weaponry.

Like this stall, rows of knives on display, some comically large and curved, like the ones in the Sinbad movies Tremont had loved as a child. Who the hell needs a knife that size in Melbourne? A woman wearing a red T-shirt with the slogan 'Make America Great Again' watched Celeste admire the sword.

At the next stall a dishwater blonde in khaki camouflage pants and a blue T-shirt fingered a pistol as a man on the other side explained how to obtain a firearm licence. She interrupted him halfway through his spiel. 'What if I don't want to do all that?'

'Go into a pub, ask around and take your chances.'

Not for the first time, Tremont calculated the odds of successfully slipping away. But the crowd wasn't thick, and he doubted he'd get far before Swain caught up with him. Indeed, the nut jobs in this place would probably cheer Swain on as he wrestled Tremont to the ground. Tremont shivered despite the humidity inside the hangar.

Swain nudged him roughly. 'This way, Carl,' he said, spitting out Tremont's first name with distain.

Celeste snickered at the pained look on Tremont's face.

The crowd thinned as they made their way to the furthest end of the hangar. Swain stopped in front of a table selling T-shirts and hoodies emblazoned with the Eureka flag emblem and slogans, like 'Fuck off, we're full' and 'Australia: love it or leave it'. Behind the table stood a skinny young man in a tight-fitting black bomber jacket with a crew cut, glued to a mobile phone.

'Hey, what do you think you're up to?' said Swain aggressively. 'These bloody T-shirts aren't going to sell themselves.'

The man looked up belligerently from his mobile. His face cracked into a grin when he saw Swain.

'Swain, you old bastard, good to see you.'

'Same, Mudcrab, same. How's the T-shirt business?'

The young man gave a despondent shrug.

'Well, don't worry mate, I got something cooking.'

Swain did a quick round of introductions. 'You got a place the three of us can hold up while we work this operation out?'

'The three of you can stay at mine, sure man.' Mudcrab's gaze lingered unenthusiastically on Tremont as he spoke. Tremont stared back, clocked the younger man's acne scars and pasty appearance. A mass of blue ink seeped from the exposed skin on his neck and hands.

Mudcrab's place was a red brick flat deep in Melbourne's northern suburbs. It had filthy carpet, a sour smell, furniture that appeared to have been rescued from the side of the road, including the bench seats from the back of a car acting as a sofa. A large Eureka flag hung on the loungeroom wall next to a slightly smaller American Confederate flag.

Celeste worked on dinner in the kitchen while Swain and Mudcrab swapped gossip over beers. The talk mainly concerned the internecine personality and political conflicts within the bewildering array of groups who made up Melbourne's far right scene, all of which, reading between the lines, were small enough to meet in a phone booth.

Mudcrab became particularly animated as he described his efforts to secure an off-the-grid bush property where like-minded groups could train for the coming race war, without any prying questions from the 'alphabets', as he referred to law enforcement agencies like the Australian Federal Police.

Tremont tried to act like he wasn't listening. He was nervous that the more he knew about their plans, ridiculous as they were, the less inclined Mudcrab and Swain would be to let him go.

'Hey Swain, you want to chill out with some nangs while we wait for dinner?'

Tremont, who prided himself on having some standards when it came to leisure drugs, considered nangs, small canisters of nitrous oxide which you inhaled to achieve a short high, beneath him. That said, they made everything hilarious for thirty seconds, so given his circumstances, maybe not such a bad idea after all.

'You going to have to drop that shit, mate, you want to hang with me,' said Swain, from his position lounging on one of the car seats.

'Yeah, sure, man, whatever you say.'

'No drugs, okay? You've got to stay strong.' Swan took a long pull on his beer. 'No room for cultural deviants, like Carl here.'

Mudcrab snickered conspiratorially, glad for the chance to deflect attention from himself.

'Yeah, what are you anyway man, an Arab or something?'

'My parents were Italian.'

'Leave him alone, Mudcrab. He has his uses, don't you Carl?'

Tremont flashed a weak smile, as Celeste entered bringing plates of steaming unidentifiable food.

After he'd finished eating, Mudcrab set his empty plate on the floor and stood up. 'Hey, Swain, you want to see something real interesting?'

Before Swain could answer, Mudcrab disappeared into an adjoining room, reappearing a few moments later holding a large cardboard box.

'Melbourne's cops have been cracking down on guns due to the local Lebanese and Turks thinking they're big tough gangsters and shooting each other.' He put the box on the floor, reached into it. 'Getting so a white man can't procure the means to protect himself.'

Mudcrab lifted up what looked to Tremont like a toy machine gun.

'Got this from a mate up north, homemade, modelled on an Uzi.'

He cocked the weapon, held it expectantly in front of Swain.

'Works and all, fires five hundred rounds a minute.'

Swain pushed off Celeste, who was lounging against his good shoulder, put his plate down, started to reach for the gun, when there was a loud knock on the front door.

'You expecting company, Mudcrab?'

The young man shook his head.

Another knock, harder.

'Put that fucking thing away,' he hissed at Mudcrab. Swain nudged Celeste. 'Go and see who's at the door.'

Swain arched his back forward, reached behind him, took out his Browning 9mm from where it had been resting at the base of his spine, took off the safety, slid it back.

Tremont heard the door open, the low murmur of voices, then noise that sounded like some sort of scuffle. Swain was only half out of his chair when Celeste came into the room, hunched slightly forward, her arm held behind her back by a tall man Tremont had never seen before.

'Evening ladies,' he said with a tone of mock civility.

He stood in the middle of the room, still holding Celeste. 'Everyone back in their seats.'

When everyone had complied, he let go of Celeste. Scowling, she rubbed her arm and sat on the floor next to Swain.

Tremont appraised the new arrival. He looked in good shape for his age. Thinning sandy hair, hard blue eyes that scanned his surroundings with an undisguised disdain. There was something about him that was comfortable being in charge, ex-military, maybe a former cop.

He fixed his gaze on Mudcrab. 'What's your name son?'

'Mudcrab.'

'What kind of fucking name is Mudcrab? Whatever, you boys need to learn how to cover your tracks a bit better. Blind Freddy could've followed you here. 'This your place?'

'Yeah.'

'Would it kill you to clean up a bit?'

'The only thing I feel like cleaning up around here is you, granddad.'

'Son, you should never make threats you can't carry out.'

Mudcrab leapt from his chair and grabbed hold of the old man's slicker.

With a fluid movement the old man suddenly had a metal baton in his hand, moved so Mudcrab's outstretched arm lay in the crook of his elbow and the baton lay across it. The old man slid his other hand under Mudcrab's arm, gripped the end of the baton and used it to push him onto his knees.

'What the fuck,' squealed Mudcrab. The old man tightened his grip, pushed Mudcrab further towards the floor, left him there as he addressed Swain.

'My name is Hardigan. I saw you and the other bloke here,' he nodded in Tremont's direction, 'casing out that apartment in the city earlier today.'

'I don't know what you mean—.'

'Don't muck me around son. You may as well have put up a billboard it was that obvious. Followed you to Flemington Racecourse and then here. Thought we might have a chat.'

Swain wiped his hands on his sides. Tremont could tell he was deliberating about whether to go for his gun.

'I'm listening,' said Swain.

'That's more like it.' Hardigan smiled, released Mudcrab from the hold he had him in. As he did, he pushed against him with one foot, sent him crashing into a flimsy coffee table which splintered apart under his weight.

'You're interested in the woman, Leigh, and so am I.' Hardigan pushed the baton against the nearest wall to fold it shut as he spoke. 'I propose an alliance.'

'I don't need any more partners.'

'Well-oiled criminal operation like this, course not.' Hardigan flicked a withering look at Mudcrab, ran a hand through his thinning hair. 'Let me ask you a question, son. What's your interest in Leigh?'

'Revenge.'

'You don't know what the fuck you've stumbled across do

you?'

'What do you mean?' said Swain uncertainly.

'Revenge is one thing. How'd you like to make twenty million dollars on top of it.

'What the hell are you going on about?'

'Get me one of these beers and all will be revealed.'

BROTHERLY LOVE

ONE

Chance's plane landed at New York's JFK Airport just before midnight. The grogginess of the long-haul flight lifted the moment he disembarked, replaced by a surge of adrenaline at the prospect of having to clear immigration.

As used as he was to the apprehension that gripped him whenever he had to deal with any kind of officialdom, Chance was unprepared for the next level security on casual display throughout the terminal. Crew cut, clenched jawed police and alert looking homeland security officials prowled the harshly lit building. They reminded Chance of the marines he'd seen guarding American facilities in Kabul, strangers in occupied territory, constantly on alert for signs of anything out of the ordinary.

Instead of passing through a body scanner, as was the practice in Australia, Chance had to step into a large clear plastic cylinder. An official told him to stand on the outline of two yellow feet affixed to the ground and put his hands in the air. 'Don't let your hands touch your head, sir,' he said. The cylinder spun around, like something out of a science fiction film.

When his turn came, Chance slid his passport and immigration form across a counter to the immigration official. The man started to tap away on the console in front of him, his eyes darting between Chance, the screen, and the passport.

The document in the name of 'John Egan' was part of a new

identity built for Chance by a Thai gangster in return for Chance's promise to bury incriminating photographs of the man's involvement in an unspeakable crime. The Thai was a computer genius, which made it all the more bizarre Chance's last memory of him was in a makeshift jungle camp, where Chance had briefly been held captive, next to a fast-flowing chocolate brown river on the Thai-Burma border. A past job, cross and double cross, had left Chance with a new face and a case of malaria he'd never been able to shake. But the passport and the identity had always stood up. Chance gave a silent prayer it would continue to.

A green light briefly illuminated Chance's hand as he pressed it against a screen in front of him and he stared into the orb-like camera which took his photo. As his prints and image raced down cables to some nameless database the size and power of which he could scarcely imagine, not for the first time, it struck Chance, as someone who made his living as a thief, he had a woefully inadequate understanding of computers and technology.

'What is the nature of your visit to the United States?' the immigration official asked without taking his eyes away from his screen.

Trying to find a man called George Mundy. A criminal, a participant in Australia's most famous heist, maybe a spy. A man who in all probability was long dead but, because there was a gossamer thin thread of a possibility he was still alive and might lead them to ninety million dollars in diamonds, Chance had come to America to find. And because of nothing more than a hunch by an embittered daughter and a photograph in an old newspaper. It sounded ridiculous when Chance thought about it, and he had to repress the urge then and there to turn around and take the first plane back to Melbourne.

'Holiday,' he said.

The official didn't reply, tapped something into his computer. Chance felt a stab of panic in his stomach that at any moment he'd be asked to step into a side room and hard-faced men and women would strip away his fake identity and leave it in shreds on the lino floor.

After a long pause, which the immigration official spent glued to his screen, Chance was finally waved through. He waited at the baggage carousel, his mind alert for any sign he might be walking into a trap.

The feeling lingered as he exited the terminal into the humid night and flagged a taxi to take him into Manhattan.

TWO

His body clock scrambled by the flight, Chance slept until early afternoon, then roamed the area around his hotel near the Hudson River, Greenwich Village, the Meatpacking District and Soho. The names were vaguely familiar from the countless American crime films Chance had watched over the years, but gentrification had sanded away all the grittiness they had exhibited on the screen, replaced it with a smooth veneer of condominiums, upmarket bars and restaurants, full of sleek, well-dressed people.

It was hot, and Chance was sweating when he finally located what he was looking for, a bar deep in the Village. The red neon sign in the window was no doubt designed to make it appear as it must have looked back in the nineteen fifties, when, according to the webpage he'd consulted before leaving his hotel, it had been a well-known hangout for Beatnik writers and poets.

Just after seven in the evening, a smattering of people were eating at tables generously spaced around the large interior. Most of the patrons were tourists, judging by the plethora of languages they spoke, who'd come for a slice of the literary history that resided in the framed black and white photographs covering the walls. Chance sat at the long wooden bar, admiring the generous selection of liquor bottles lining the wall, their contents backlit by red lighting. A baseball game was on the television, the sound turned down.

A thickset man with the florid face of a life-time drinker and greying hair tended bar. He was dressed in a short-sleeved white cotton bowling shirt; a red stripe running down one side, a patch on the other, with the word 'Marvin' in cursive script. The man Leigh had told him to talk to.

'What'll it be buddy?' Marvin said when he got to Chance.

Chance ordered a tap beer, nursed it as he watched Marvin serve customers with quick, economical movements, every interaction punctuated by a wipe of the bar top with a towel he draped over his shoulder. Marvin paused to exchange a few words with those who were presumably locals, was brusque with the tourists. Two-tier service, the way of the world.

Chance drained the weak beer, raised his glass in Marvin's direction.

'Another?' said Marvin.

Chance nodded. 'You got anything that doesn't take like piss, Marvin?'

'An Aussie, yeah?'

'That's me.'

Marvin reached behind him into a nearby cooler, lifted out a frosted bottle, and flipped the lid with an opener on a piece of string attached to the bar. He poured a dark, rich liquid into a glass and set it in front of Chance. The bartender placed both his large hands on the bar, watched as Chance took a large pull of the beer.

'That's better.'

'Can I get you anything else?'

'How about some information?'

Marvin narrowed his eyes, leaned against the cooler, slowly wiping his hands with the towel.

'About what?'

He was a big man, overweight without looking soft. Chance kept his eyes on his large hands.

'Salvatore Luchese.'

'He a writer, in one of those pictures on the wall?' Marvin smirked at his own joke. 'We get a lot of tourists coming in, asking about old writers, as if the fuck I'd know.'

'Don't think so, not unless he was writing in the eighties, maybe something about the roofers union in Philadelphia?'

'City of brotherly love, or so I hear.' Marvin smiled. 'Ain't been there in a long time.'

After several moments, Marvin broke off Chance's gaze, went to the end of the bar, made a phone call, his back to Chance. He put down the receiver, came back.

'Buddy, we close at midnight. Come back then.'

Chance sat in a diner across the street, keeping an eye on the bar as he worked his way through a rubbery hamburger and a cup of bitter coffee. Just after midnight, the red neon in the bar's front window went dark. Chance left some money on the table, crossed the road. He pressed against the bar's front door. It opened, and he went inside.

Marvin stood behind the counter, illuminated by a row of downlights above him. He glanced up from the glass he was polishing, smiled at his visitor.

Chance had only taken a couple of steps when he felt a jolt of intense pain near his left calf. His legs buckled, and he fell to the ground.

Chance gasped, stretched out his leg and breathed in beer fumes from the polished concrete floor. The area around the knee throbbed, like a bad cramp, but nothing was broken.

He rolled onto his back, his vision full of tiny lights, like the sparks from a wood fire given a good prod. A wiry youth emerged from the shadows, a baseball bat in one hand.

'He moves, hit him again, harder,' Marvin said over his shoulder as he locked the front door from the inside.

Chance grimaced at the pain. 'They told me New York was a tough town.'

'It used to be a tough town, buddy,' said Marvin, crouching down, undoing the laces from Chance's sneakers and tying them together. Now it's just full of douchebags and nosey arseholes like you.'

Marvin gave Chance a rough frisk, moving him from side to side with ease until satisfied he wasn't armed, then withdrew the wallet from one of the side pockets of Chance's jeans.

'Okay, Mister John Egan,' Marvin said reading from Chance's false driver's licence, 'let's you, me and my friend here go for a little talk.'

Marvin picked Chance up by both feet, dragged him behind the bar, down a short corridor, and into a small room lit by a bare globe on a chord. Boxes and crates lined the walls, surrounding a small space with an old orange plastic bucket seat at its centre.

The pain in his leg was bad but not debilitating, and Chance thought about resisting. He might have been able to take one, but not both his assailants. He let Marvin sit him in the chair, waited for the opportunity to try and talk his way out of the situation he'd got himself in.

The youth stood in the doorway, tapping the bat into the palm of his hand, as Marvin picked up a large roll of black gaffer tape on a nearby box. He wound it around Chance half a dozen times, reached into his jeans pocket, withdrew a box cutter, pushed the blade out and cut the tape off.

'Now you listen to me, you Aussie cocksucker, I don't appreciate some guy with a hard face, looks like it's been places, walking into my place of employment and throwing around the names of people I ain't heard of for a long time and frankly, would be happy if I never heard again.'

Marvin placed the tip of the box cutter blade on the soft flesh under Chance's right eye. Chance winced as Marvin made a short cut.

'Believe me, buddy, that's as good as it's going to get.' Marvin held the blade in front of Chance's face. 'Now it's time to start talking. Who the hell are you, and what the hell do you want? You got thirty seconds.'

'Listen to me.' Chance tried not to panic as he felt a rivulet of blood run down his cheek. 'A woman named Leigh, Vera Leigh, said to come and see you on my way to Philadelphia. She said you could help me out with contacts, information, be useful to me there.'

Marvin lowered the knife, looked at Chance askance. 'Another name I haven't heard in a long time. She still alive?'

'Very much so and she wanted me to ask whether you still own that brown Mercury Cyclone, with the leopard skin patterned seat covers.'

'My first wife took it in our divorce. I loved that goddamn car.' Marvin's brow furrowed. 'What's your connection to Vera?'

'I work for her.'

'How do I know you ain't lying?'

Chance did a quick mental calculation, just after midnight in New York, around two in the afternoon in Melbourne. Leigh would be taking calls. If she was sober enough. He recited Leigh's private mobile number to Marvin, told him to call it. Repeated it to make sure he had it right, prayed Leigh picked up.'

Chance saw Marvin weighing up the information. He retracted the boxcutter's blade, put it back in his jeans pocket. 'Woody, watch this prick while I go make a call.'

When Marvin walked back in the room, he took out the boxcutter and sliced away the tape. Chance stretched his leg, the pain now a dull throb, dabbed at the cut under his eye, felt dried blood.

'Thanks a bunch, Woody, you can go now,' said Marvin.

Woody grinned at Chance. 'Hey buddy, no hard feelings.'

Marvin watched as Chance untied his shoelaces, wavering slightly as he stood.

'Let me buy you a drink, Gary.'

THREE

Chance drained his shot glass. Bourbon, not his preferred drink, but when in Rome.

Marvin had turned off all the lights above the bar, save one. They sat in the single pool of light. Chance savoured the stillness.

'I'm sure sorry about your leg, Gary.' Marvin's face had softened, appeared almost fatherly as he topped up their shot glasses. 'Mind if I have one of these?' He gestured to Chance's pouch of rolling tobacco on the bar top.

'Sure was good to talk to Vera,' he said as his thick fingers started to roll a cigarette with surprising dexterity. 'She sounded a little loaded, to be honest, but that's no surprise, she always was a wild one. Well, last time I saw her almost fifty years ago.'

The night's events further confirmed Leigh was getting sloppy. Like not reaching out in advance to Marvin to let him know to expect a visitor. Chance made a mental note he would have to lift his own game to make up for the slack.

The pain in his leg had subsided to a dull throb, and he was in no mood to reminisce but could see value in getting any useful background Marvin might offer on his mysterious employer.

'Where'd you meet Vera?' Chance asked.

'The first time, right? Let's see, that'd be Kings Cross, Sydney, some titty club, the Red something.' Marvin lit his cigarette with a match from a book, shook it out with an exaggerated movement as he strained for the name. 'The Red Baron. That was the one.

'I was a dumb nineteen-year-old from a dead-end Pennsylvanian steel town who'd joined the Marines to see the world. What I ended up seeing was a whole lot of shit in Vietnam. Vera was a fresh faced eighteen-year-old from some place in country Queensland, who had come to the big smoke and washed up as go-go dancer at the Red Baron.'

Marvin took a slug from his drink.

'Anyway, I was on R&R and wanted some company. She wanted my American dollars, plenty of which I had, and a good time. And, boy, did we have it. She rented a flat in Kings Cross with a couple of girlfriends. We had some great parties there.

'A lot of the Australian broads, we used to call them "grasshoppers", they'd take us GIs down to the big park in the centre of Sydney, where they'd have a friend or two waiting to roll you. Not Vera. She just wanted to have fun, and I was happy to oblige. I came back a couple more times during the war, and always hung with Vera. And she visited me in America once, much to the anger of my then wife. Anyway, the worst it ever got in Sydney was a bit of grass and some speed—black bombers, I think you Aussies used to call them. It all felt pretty innocent until smack started appearing on the scene.'

Marvin stared into the darkness over Chance's shoulder a moment, nodded his head slightly, brought his focus back to his companion.

'Vera didn't say too much about what you want over the phone. She just asked me to help you. For old time's sake. Okay, so, what do you want?'

Chance gave him a quick precis of what he knew about Mundy, omitting any mention of the diamonds. As he spoke, he withdrew a folded enlarged photocopy of the picture that had accompanied the article in the Philadelphia newspaper showing Mundy opening the door for the mob guy Luchese. The blown-up image accentuated the half tone dot effect of the newsprint, made it look slightly blurry, but it was all he had to go on. He pushed the paper across the bar to Marvin.

The barman stroked his chin as he stared at it. 'This guy opening the door, the Australian you say you're looking for. I don't recall him.'

He mashed the remains of his cigarette into the ashtray, placed a finger on the face of the man getting out of the car. 'But this arsehole, yeah, I remember him real good.'

Marvin poured himself another drink, made to do the same for Chance, but Chance put his hand over his glass. He'd already be jetlagged tomorrow; he didn't need a hangover as well.

'I worked for Luchese back in the day.'

'Doing what?'

'This and that, mainly collecting debts, occasionally something a bit rougher.' He took another drink, let the implication sink in. 'Look, I'd been back from 'Nam several years. There was no work in the town I grew up in, so I came to Philly. One thing led to another. I met a guy in this bar I used to hang out in, he hooked me up with Luchese's people. I made some money and developed a nasty smack habit.' Marvin shifted on his bar stool. 'I ain't proud of that time, but you do what you gotta do, right?'

'No judgement from me,' Chance looked him in the eyes as he spoke. 'You clean now?'

'Twenty-eight years last month.'

Cheers raised his glass. 'More power to you, Marvin.'

'*Slainte*,' said Marvin, returning the toast. 'A lot of these mob guys were scumbags who'd sell their own mothers if there was a dime to be made, but Salvatore was a real next level piece of shit.'

'That picture was taken outside his court case for the murder of his predecessor as president of Local 30 of the Philadelphia Roofers Union,' said Chance.

'The Sonny Rosata slaying, yeah, I remember that.' Marvin looked at the grainy picture anew. 'That was what, late '86, early '87?'

'January '87. Chance rolled a cigarette, hoped the nicotine would stave off the exhaustion nipping at his brain.

'Yeah, Luchese killed him with a shotgun, from memory, in the basement of Rosata's own home. Double barrel, up close. Forensics had to pick bits of Rosata off the furniture upholstery to ID him. Luchese had enough money to pay someone to do the hit but enjoyed doing the scut work himself. That's the kind of guy we're talking about.'

'Did he beat the charge?'

'Does a fucking bear shit in the woods? Yeah, the main prosecution witness who could put Luchese in the same street Rosata lived in on the night of the killing suddenly developed serious amnesia.'

Marvin drained his glass, followed it up by wiping his hand across his mouth. 'You'd reckon I'd notice something like an Australian hanging about Luchese, but nada on that score.' Marvin shook his head in self-recrimination. 'But that's the same time I was having an on and off relationship with the smack, so my memory of those years is not as reliable as it might be. Plus, the early eighties, you know, it was a fucked-up time. A lot of instability in the Philly crime scene.'

'I was at school,' said Chance, lighting his cigarette.

'Long time boss, guy by the name of Angelo Bruno, pretty much ran the place in the sixties and seventies. Then he got hit sometime in 1980, triggered a major mob war over territory.'

Marvin poured himself another shot, downed half of it.

'Luchese had been a Bruno lieutenant, but after the hit sided with a guy called Nicodemo "Little Nicky" Scarfo, who ran things for most of the eighties. Nicky was a greedy little prick, started leaning on everyone for more money. Plus, that was around the time the mob got into smack in a big way, which meant more money and more violence. Civilians started getting caught in the crossfire. That drew the attention of the cops and the FBI, who frankly had been happy to look the other way as long as the Outfit tucked everything in tight.

'Anyway, it all went to shit. New York got involved, the body count went up, mob guys started cutting deals with the

Feds, you know what I mean?'

'I've seen the movies, yeah.'

Marvin paused his glass in mid-air for a moment, like he was trying to figure out whether Chance was making fun of him or not, let it pass, and drained his glass.

'Scarfo went to jail, and some guy called Merlino took over. Still runs the place from a condo in Florida. Can you believe it?'

'And Luchese?'

'Don't know, I had to leave town in a hurry due to a disagreement I had one night, came to New York, been here ever since.'

'This bar, you own it?'

'You reckon I'd be tending bar in my seventies if I owned this place?' Marvin looked at him askance. 'Nah, that'd be the thirty-something-year-old college-educated guy who made a motza out of something to do with computers and has a fondness for Jack Kerouac. If I had the money, I'd be down in Florida too, enjoying the sunshine.'

'You wouldn't happen to know whether Luchese is still alive?'

'No, but I can find out.' Marvin stood, his signal the discussion was at an end. 'Luchese would be well into his eighties, if he was still kicking. I wouldn't put it past him. He was mean enough to stare death in the eye without blinking. Come back the same time tomorrow night. And scout's honour, no baseball bats this time.'

FOUR

'Luchese is still alive,' Marvin had said as Chance took a stool at the bar counter the next night. 'A spritely eighty-five. And with the number of fucking enemies he has, can you believe it? Prick'll probably outlive me.'

Marvin set up two shot glasses, poured them both drinks, downed his in one gulp.

'How do I find him?' said Chance, sipping his.

'I still have one or two friends in Philly. Take this.' Marvin handed Chance a cheap burner phone. 'I've put one number into it. When you arrive in Philadelphia, text it. The person who'll respond, Jez, will show you around town, help you deal with any angry locals.'

'What if I don't need any help?'

'Last night says different. How's the leg by the way?'

'I'll live.'

'You want to stay that way, I suggest you engage Jez's services. Believe me, friend, it'll be worth the cost.'

Chance started to argue, but Marvin cut him off with a raised hand.

'I may be just a dumb bartender, but it doesn't take a genius to figure out whatever you want this Mundy guy for, there's money at the end of it, usually is when Vera's concerned.'

Marvin gave himself a refill.

'Don't get me wrong, Gary. I don't want a slice. This one is for old times' sake, you know, for Vera. But Jez is a professional and professionals get paid.'

Chance drained his glass, warming to the taste of bourbon. Vera had dispatched him to America with ample finances, so paying Jez wasn't the problem. But Chance preferred to work alone—or at the very least know who he was partnering with.

'If it makes any difference, I can vouch for Jez, one hundred and ten per cent.'

Chance realised that to disagree further would be an insult to Marvin. He motioned his glass for a refill to seal the deal.

'Got something else for you,' Marvin said after he refreshed their drinks. He took something from under the counter, slid it across the bar. A small pistol in a leather ankle holster.

'Ruger LCP, what we used to call a Saturday night special back in the day. Most common handgun in America, six rounds, one in the chamber. This one is clean as a whistle.'

'Only belonged to a little old lady who fired it on Sunday,' said Chance, not bothering to argue.

Marvin's face broke into a paternal grin. 'Something like that. Not long-range, but the gun you want when you don't want anyone to know you have a gun. You know how to use this?'

He nodded, rolled himself a cigarette.

'They call Philly the City of Brotherly Love,' said Marvin, reaching for the tobacco. 'But love hurts, you know what I'm saying? So, best be prepared.'

Chance took the Amtrak from New York to Philadelphia. He spent the ninety-minute journey staring at the passing scenery, fascinated by how quickly the neighbourhoods turned from prosperous, large houses on well-tended blocks, to run-down, dilapidated buildings with overgrown yards full of old cars and abandoned white goods. The two Americas were subdivided by shopping complexes and strip malls.

It was mid-morning when he exited 30th Street Station,

climbed into a taxi, and gave the address of a large hotel in the city's central business district. The driver, who looked like he hailed from somewhere in Eastern Europe, was completely encased in thick Perspex. The only opening to the passenger area was a slit of about a foot in length, through which Chance passed the fare when they arrived at his destination.

Chance made it a practice to always avoid hotels in the sketchier parts of town if he could. Those places attracted the kind of people who, in turn, attracted the police. His preference was always for establishments which catered to the fleeting business trade, staffed by people skilled at making disinterest seem like deference.

Chance was dozing in his hotel room when the mobile phone on the bedside table next to him pinged. Jez's return text told him to be at a place called the Veteran Boxers Association in Port Richmond, a neighbourhood on the eastern edge of the city near the Delaware River, at 4pm.

Chance arrived early, told the cab driver to pull over several blocks away from the meeting place. He walked the rest of the way to take in the surroundings. A former industrial area by the look of it, the factories were long closed, but Port Richmond still had a working class feel Chance associated with the suburb of Melbourne's inner west that he'd grown up in.

It was a sensation accentuated by the late afternoon light, which made everything look slightly frayed. Street after street of two-or-three storey brown brick row and weatherboard houses, broken up with the occasional small business, delis, hairdressers and bars. A heavy Polish presence, if the number of diners and shops flying the red-and-white-striped flag was anything to go by.

The Association was in an unassuming double-storey red brick box building on the corner of two side streets near the Port of Philadelphia. He pushed open the glass door with 'VBA Ring' in cursive gold lettering on it. Inside was a large room, blue-and-white-chequered linoleum floor, tables and chairs in two rows.

Every inch of wall space was covered with decades of Philadelphia boxing history. A visual kaleidoscope of a century of sweat, pain, loss and triumph in the ring; muscular white, black and brown male bodies posing in their shorts and gloves, fight posters, ringside shots, newspaper clippings, everything neatly framed. Some of the material was recent, but the majority was yellowed with age.

Rest rooms ran off one side, the other opened onto a long, narrow room with a wooden bar running along one wall, red vinyl stools along the length of it. The opposite wall was covered in more memorabilia.

Say what you want about America, Chance mused as he took a stool, the place knows how to do bars. The only other customers, an elderly man and woman, ignored him, their attention glued to a baseball game broadcast on a large flatscreen TV.

Chance ordered a shot of bourbon from the aging barman with a craggy face dominated by a nose which had obviously been broken multiple times and never properly reset.

'Mug like yours, I figure you might have done a few rounds in your time,' said a female voice.

Chance turned around to face a compact-looking woman in black jeans and a light bomber jacket standing behind him.

'You could say that, but not in the ring.'

She slid onto the stool next to him.

'I don't mean to imply you're the ugliest man alive, but you better hope he doesn't die.' She chuckled at her own joke, signalled the bartender with an upturned finger.

'You make a habit of coming up to strange men and disparaging their appearance?'

'Only my potential employers.'

The barmen came over, an affectionate smile on his face. 'The usual, Jez?'

The woman nodded. 'Yeah, Tony.'

'Jez?'

'Jezebel.' My father had a sense of humour, or so he liked to think. A trait shared by Marvin, who gets a kick referring people to me without revealing all the details.'

The barman placed a glass in front of her, made small talk while he poured a shot of tequila. Chance checked her reflection in the mirror behind the bar. Mid-to-late twenties, if he had to put an age to her. Cropped red hair, the same colour as the riot of freckles on her face, a mouth set in an intelligent smirk.

His own face stared back at him next to hers. Askew nose, square, boxy face, pronounced jawline, short back and sides haircut, the fresh plaster where Marvin had cut him.

'He's up on the wall over there,' she said.

'Who?'

'My old man, Fergus McClusky, there's a picture of him on the wall. Philadelphia Police middleweight champion three years running. She raised her glass, drained it in one gulp.

'That why you like this place?'

'Yeah, Something like that. Let's just say it's my second office.'

Her large brown eyes suddenly became serious.

'Well, Mister Egan, shall we get down to business? Marvin told me you have an interest in our wonderful city's Italian culture.'

'Yes.'

'And you needed a driver to see the sights and possible protection during your stay.'

'Marvin seemed to think so.'

Jez's freckles danced as she grimaced. 'Marvin's say-so is usually enough to sway a potential client, but I can see you need additional convincing.' She rummaged in the inside pocket of her bomber jacket, withdrew a leather wallet, opened it in front of him.

'This good enough?' she said, her voice sharp with irritation.

Chance made a show of closely examining her ID. The words 'Private Investigator' in blue stood out, along with a mug shot that made her look like a juvenile criminal offender.

It's not hard to put together a fake ID, thought Chance. He

would know.

As if reading his mind, she grabbed it off him, snapped it shut.

'Look, I got to eat like everyone else. I can drive, and while I may not look like Rocky Balboa, I can look after myself and maybe even you.'

Chance had a feeling she wasn't finished, said nothing.

'Now Mister Egan, or whatever your name is, can we please cut the bullshit. Are you interested in employing my services or not? Because if not, I've got a criminology term paper to finish.'

Chance put his hand out.

'And what do I pay for the privilege?' he said as she shook it.

'You know what they say, you got to ask you can't afford it.'

FIVE

A red-and-white-striped pole in a glass case indicated the single fronted building had once been a barber shop. The venetian blinds on the front window were closed, and a dozen thick-set men, dressed for the heat in shorts and T-shirts, milled around outside the front, smoking and talking.

Jez had described today's outing as strictly a reconnoitre. 'We watch from a distance and don't do anything.'

She and Chance sat a block away in her car. The vehicle, a red Chevy Malibu, a common car if the number Chance had seen on the roads was anything to go by, attracted no attention.

Her car was clean of the usual detritus Chance associated with working vehicles, except for a stack of folders and textbooks on the back seat. He tried to catch the titles without being intrusive. Something about defunding the police, another about prison reform.

Jez hadn't been lying about her driving skills. She'd picked him up outside his hotel at precisely the prearranged time, manoeuvred the car with ease through the city's chaotic midmorning traffic. Chance savoured the knot of tension in his stomach that arrived whenever a job kicked into gear, paid close attention to where they were going. She drove down a main thoroughfare called Passyunk Avenue, eventually turning off into a side street. A brief snatch of affluence for several blocks before the surroundings turned light industrial—

automotive repair shops, warehouses and wholesale dealers—and she parked on a side street.

'Luchese spends most of his days farting into a couch in front of the TV.' Jez lay back in the driver's seat, pushed her Ray Bans up her nose as she spoke. 'But he still has one or two business interests, a few no-show jobs in the roofer's union, a loan shark business run by his son.'

'Just another working American family trying to get by in these tough times.'

'Something like that.'

'So, those guys out the front, they supposed to be hardworking roofers? The shape most of them are in, they look like they haven't swung a hammer in a while.'

'It's all the cold cuts they eat,' said Jez.

'*Gabagool*? Ovah here,' said Chance in an exaggerated American gangster accent.

A slight smile creased the corner of Jez's mouth. 'Get me started on jokes from *The Sopranos*, we'll be here all day. Anyway, Wednesdays and Fridays, Luchese leaves the house to have lunch at this social club.'

'That what this is?'

'Yeah, neutral territory away from the interminable beefs and grievances these guys always seem to have brewing, a place where they can hang out, drink coffee and play cards. Works like a safety valve, helps keep everything cool. You don't expect no surprises, everyone knows who everyone is and who they are tight with.'

A visible ripple went through the crowd of men as a black SUV with tinted windows pulled up.

'Heads up,' said Jez, sitting up. 'Show time.'

First out of the SUV was the driver, a tall, funereal looking man in a black suit and open-necked white shirt, a narrow, angular face under a head of thinning dark hair.

'That's Vinnie "The Wire" Angellini, Luchese's long time bodyguard. The old man never goes anywhere in public without him.'

The rear door facing the street opened and a youngish man stepped out.

'That's his son, Michael,' said Jez.

Luchese Junior wore a tight-fitting dress shirt and jeans. He had tanned skin, a well-sculpted face with a carefully maintained five o'clock shadow, framed by a generous mane of wavy jet-black hair. A showy streak was evidenced by the chunky gold watch visible on his wrist. He had a Bluetooth piece in one ear against which he pressed a finger while carrying on an animated conversation.

'I hate flashy guys with Bluetooth,' said Chance. 'Does Luchese Junior have a nickname?'

'How about shit bird?'

Chance was starting to like his companion.

The bodyguard held the door open, and an elderly man stepped out. Despite the heat, Salvatore Luchese dressed in a brown knit cardigan and a flat woollen cap, a pair of dark sunglasses one size too large for his face. He appeared shaky and slightly hesitant, before he got his bearings and stood erect as he could in front of his troops.

Luchese Junior, having finished his conversation, engaged in a series of exaggerated hugs and back slaps with several of the men on the footpath. The rest of the crowd formed into a rough semi-circle around his father. He gave off a sour, aloof vibe, a cranky relative at a family gathering he didn't want to attend.

'They sure do make a fuss of the old guy,' said Chance, shifting in his seat.

'If you can't be respected, settle for fear,' replied Jez, as the men, led by Luchese senior, filed into the building.

'What's that?'

'Something my pop used to say.'

'Was he talking about the gangsters or cops?'

'Both.'

As the last man disappeared inside, Jez turned to Chance.

'Salvatore Luchese didn't get to be eighty-five by letting strangers waltz up, introduce themselves, and start talking. Especially when the conversation topic is an old associate from a turbulent time, who might be linked to an old beef. All that approach will get you is a bullet in the back of the head the minute you step through his door.'

'So, what's the plan?'

'You want to do this? There's a protocol, okay? You tell me why you want to meet Luchese. I make some phone calls, talk to some people who know people and maybe, and I stress, maybe, you get to talk to the old man.'

'Let's do it.'

SIX

Having heard nothing from Jez in twenty-four hours, Chance was contemplating calling her when his burner rang.

'It's on for later tonight,' she said without preamble.

Chance listened as she ran through the instructions. Luchese's son as the intermediary, would pick Chance up at a pre-arranged location and take him to meet his father.

'Sounds very complicated for such a straightforward request,' Chance said when she had finished.

'These guys raise artifice to a high art. It's connected to all this respect bullshit they go on about. Seriously, play it cool, go through the motions, you'll get your face time with Luchese. Everything has been smoothed over, and there'll be no trouble. But in the event anything goes wrong, I'll be nearby. Be at the address I gave you tonight and don't be late.'

The location was outside a run-down bar in the northeast part of Philadelphia, on the corner of a deserted stretch of intersection, directly under an elevated railway line. The bar's faded green exterior was oddly colour coordinated with the paint job on the steel girders supporting the rail track. A tramp in a frayed army jacket paced backwards and forwards outside, mumbling the word 'fucker' again and again.

A dull glow emanated through a pane of bevelled glass at the entrance. Chance cracked the door, spied a smattering of souls sitting at a long wooden bar, Keno on the television fixed to the wall.

Chance glanced at his watch. Fifteen minutes past ten and no sign of Luchese Junior. No sign of Jez, either, but he didn't expect to see her. The fact the location was so far away from Luchese's modest brick house in South Philly made Chance uneasy.

He felt cold, despite the warm evening, put both hands into the pockets of his denim jacket, cursed George Mundy under his breath. A train thundered overhead, causing the tramp to mutter faster until it had passed.

Five minutes later, a pair of headlights slowly turned into the street and approached him. As they came closer, Chance recognised the same make of SUV as the one that had delivered Luchese senior to his social club a couple of days before.

A tinted back window wound down as the vehicle pulled up in front of Chance to reveal the face of Luchese's bodyguard, Vinnie "The Wire" Angellini.

'Get in Mister Egan,' he said in a surprisingly delicate voice.

Chance flicked the rollie he was smoking into the darkness, climbed inside, and was immediately hit by a blast of air-conditioning mixed with cologne. Luchese Junior sat in the front passenger seat, bathed in a blue light from the car's elaborate dashboard. The driver, a man Chance hadn't seen before, glanced at him in the rear-view mirror.

Luchese Junior turned slightly as the car pulled away, a smirk on his face. 'Sit back and relax, Mister Egan, we're taking the long way.'

They were either being careful, or it was a deliberate ploy to disorientate him. Whatever the case, there wasn't much Chance would do. He sat back, scoped out the inside of the car. The interior was spotless.

'Does your dad know you've taken his ride?'

Luchese Junior said nothing, but Chance felt Angellini tense next to him.

'Hey, I'm just breaking balls, isn't that what you guys say all the time?' He addressed the question to Angellini, who didn't respond. The bodyguard was older than Chance had first made him, wisps of grey in his thinning hair.

An alarm went off in Chance's head as they crossed a large bridge over what looked like the Delaware River, a refinery lit up stadium-like on the other side, flare stacks intermittently belching fire into the night sky. They were leaving the city.

'I appreciate the tour, but something tells me this is not the way to your dad's house,' Chance said, trying to keep his features impassive.

On cue, he heard the click of the automatic locking system. Angellini produced a pistol and poked it into Chance's midriff far harder than he needed to. Luchese Junior leant over the front seat, also pointing a pistol at him. His had a silencer attached.

'I thought we had an agreement. I was going to talk to your father.' A lump of fear congealed in Chance's throat. 'I don't mean any harm. I just want to ask him a few questions.'

'Don't move and shut the fuck up, you Aussie fuck.' Luchese Junior shook his head to dislodge a lock of his wavy hair falling across his forehead as he spoke. 'I don't want to do anything that would mess up the inside of pop's car.'

The driver glanced at Chance in the rear view mirror, licked his lips.

He might be able to disable Angellini, but there was no way Chance could take on the bodyguard without Luchese Junior shooting him at point blank range from the front seat. Chance just hoped Jez was half as good as she said she was and followed them.

The vehicle exited the bridge, turned off the main road, and made several sharp turns through an industrial area where the traffic thinned.

The car stopped in front of a cyclone wire fence. The headlights illuminated an uneven dirt road stretching into darkness, hulking black shapes on either side. A man with a bushy moustache in a grease-streaked white T-shirt and blue jeans, carrying a sawn-off shotgun, appeared out of the gloom, opened the gate and closed it after them.

The black shapes lining the road revealed themselves to be rows of old cars. A wrecking yard. The driver pulled into a pool of illumination created by a floodlight affixed to the front of a prefab building, killed the engine.

Once Chance had stepped out of the car, Angellini patted him down, locating the Ruger. He withdrew it from the ankle holster, threw it on the ground.

'Okay, now he's clean.'

'So, this is the guy who wants to talk to my dad about that fuck Mundy, yeah?' Luchese Junior put his face inches from Chance's. The driver, a thickset man, whose paunch strained against his long-sleeved tee shirt, stood next to him, holding a pistol casually at his side.

In addition to Angellini, Luchese Junior, and the driver, there was the gate opener, who had yet to reappear. Maybe others in the prefab building. That made at least four Chance would have to deal with. Not good odds. In his favour, none of them looked like they exactly did hard time in the gym, but with the firepower they were carrying they didn't have to.

'What the hell gives, Luchese?' said Chance, playing for time. 'I thought this had all been sorted out, that—'

A blow to the neck interrupted Chance before he could finish. Angellini had hit him with the butt of his pistol. Not hard, otherwise he'd be unconscious, but hard enough for Chance to briefly see stars in his vision.

'Shuddup, you prick,' growled Angellini behind him.

Luchese Junior bent towards him, pressed his silencer against Chance's temple.

'The only thing we got organised for you is a one-way ride with our car crusher.' He pressed harder. 'And you'll be fucking alive when we feed you to it, if you don't come clean with the real reason you're here.'

'I have no idea what you're talking about,' hissed Chance.

'Pop don't need no aggravation at his age, especially about

that *stronzo* Mundy, fuck his mother for ever bringing him into the world.' Luchese Junior spat on the ground.

Chance looked up at Luchese Junior over the barrel of the man's gun, the gangster's face backlit by the floodlight. He heard a noise on the roof of the prefab, thought he was imagining it until Luchese Junior turned around, had obviously heard it too.

It was quickly followed by the sound of a hard thump, something falling to the ground. Chance saw a shadow move at the edge of the light. Luchese Junior turned, fired as he tried to get a fix on it. The driver joined in.

Chance swivelled, brought his elbow hard as he could into where he hoped Angellini's stomach was. He connected, felt like he was punching a hard sack of sand. Chance heard a grunt of surprise as Angellini's pistol fell to the ground.

Out of the corner of his eye, Chance saw a figure emerge from the shadow and registered the driver suddenly collapsing, as if passing out.

Chance felt something slip over his head, a wire. Instinctively, he put a hand up to swat it away.

The wire tightened, biting deep into the fleshy heel of Chance's hand. He howled in pain as blood spurted out of the cut.

Chance raised his free arm, tried to aim the end of his elbow in the direction of what he hoped was Angellini's face, was successful on his third try. The wire slackened, Chance using the sudden manoeuvrability to reach his free arm around his assailant's neck and push them both down into the dirt.

The wire fell away, and Chance broke free. He stood uncertainly, blood running down his arm from the deep cut. Trying to ignore the pain, he spied Angellini's gun on the ground.

Despite his age, Angellini was fast on his feet. He held a length of wire between two dowls of wood by one end, swung the garrotte in a figure eight. Chance felt it whistle in the air in front of his face.

Chance dived towards the pistol, grabbed it with both hands, flipped onto his back, and fired. Angellini recoiled like someone had punched him, a stunned expression on his face as he looked down at his chest where he'd been shot. Chance winced in pain from the cut, fired three more times. Angellini fell to the ground and didn't move.

Chance moved into a crouch, the pain in his hand a hard throb. The driver lay in the dirt with his back to him. Luchese Junior sat on the ground, his well-groomed features now dishevelled and contorted in pain. One of his arms dangled at a slightly unnatural angle. Jez stood over him, holding a cord connected to what looked like a policeman's truncheon.

She was dressed the same as when he'd first met her, the only addition being a tight-fitting baseball cap with the head of an eagle on it, which partly cast her face in shadow.

'I guess you've figured out how Angellini got his nickname,' she said, kicking Luchese's gun away from him. 'By the way, your fee just went way up.'

'You took your sweet time,' said Chance, standing unsteadily. He looked at Angellini, his chest a mess of dark, pulpy colour, his lifeless hand still holding one of the dowls of the garrotte.

'You take those other two out by yourself?'

'My dad's old nightstick comes in handy,' she said.

She cast the cord attached to the truncheon for effect. It spun forward in front of her and snapped back into her hand. 'Neither of those boys are used to doing their own scut work, so wasn't that hard.'

'What about the guy on the gate?'

'He's back there somewhere with a busted shin.' She produced plastic cuffs from inside her jacket. Luchese Junior whelped in pain as she slowly manoeuvred his wrists together and secured the cuffs.

'I don't know what you're selling, Mister,' she said, repeating the procedure with the unconscious man. 'But whatever it is, these guys don't want to buy it.'

Chance nodded. He felt around his neck. There didn't seem to be any damage. His left hand was another story. Blood from the wound had soaked the sleeve of his denim jacket.

'I got a medical kit in my trunk,' said Jez.

'I'll watch these two while you go get their friend,' said Chance. 'After that, you can fix up my hand, then I'll need you to drive. It's time I paid a visit to Salvatore Luchese.'

SEVEN

The prefab site office contained a collection of chairs around a gunmetal desk, a matching metal filing cabinet. Chance found a half-full bottle of cheap Scotch in the bottom draw of the cabinet. He sat at the desk, sipped from the bottle as he rubbed the back of his neck where he'd been hit. The three surviving hoods, trussed up by Jez, sat on the floor in a row along the wall.

Two of the men stared blankly into space, still not quite sure what had hit them. Luchese Junior glared at Jez, his face radiating major thwarted machismo vibes at having been bested by a woman.

A car pulled up outside the office, its headlights briefly lighting up the dirty office window. Chance heard footsteps and two men entered the room, a large black man and a scrawny looking white guy with spiky bleach blonde hair. The two men acknowledged Chance, briefly surveyed the room, before falling into a hushed discussion with Jez.

The black man, whom Jez called Kyrone, left a few moments later. His companion selected the shotgun from the collection of weapons confiscated from the gangsters, checked it was loaded, took a seat, lay the gun across his knees, and watched the captives.

Chance crouched in front of Luchese Junior, jiggled the keys he'd relieved him of earlier. 'Are any of these work for the old man's house?'

The gangster avoided eye contact, said nothing. Sweat ran

down his face, a sign the pain from the broken arm was getting worse.

Chance slapped the point at which the arm was broken. Luchese Junior screamed in pain.

'Listen to me. If you'd gone through with the arrangement we'd agreed on, none of this would've happened. I would've found out what I needed and been on my way.'

Luchese Junior grimaced, glanced up at Chance, pleadingly.

'I don't want to hurt your father. I just want to talk to him. She's going to drive me to his house,' he nodded in Jez's direction, 'while her friend here keeps an eye on the three of you. When I've finished, provided I'm safe, she'll make a phone call, and you'll be kicked loose.

'Now tell me about the layout of your dad's house. And show me which of these keys will get me in.'

Salvatore Luchese lived in an unassuming brown brick row house near the Italian market in south Philadelphia. Jez inched around the block twice so Chance could clock it before making his approach. Light was visible through the curtains on the ground floor front window, a narrow laneway running along the rear.

Chance asked Jez to stop the car around the corner. He retrieved an old blanket from the boot, walked along the deserted laneway, counting the houses until he came to the rear of Luchese's. An aging timber fence, pickets cut in blunt triangles along the top, just as his son had described it.

He scoured the laneway, spied an abandoned chest of drawers a couple of houses away. He pushed the latter against the back fence, threw the blanket over the top of the pickets, clambered over.

His hand throbbed as he landed on the other side. He'd have to get the wound seen to properly, but for now, Jez's patch up—liquid stitches and a tight bandage—would have to do.

He'd declined her offer of a local anaesthetic, needing to stay sharp for just a few more hours.

Chance found himself in a square of concrete bordered by narrow strips of dirt planted with what looked like tomatoes on either side.

He'd abandoned his bloodstained denim jacket back at the wrecking yard, replaced it with an old canvas work jacket he'd found in the site office. It smelt of engine grease and sweat. He took the keys from a pocket, slid one onto the backdoor lock. It opened. He stepped inside. In his good hand, Luchese Junior's silenced Glock .45 swept the room.

From a neat kitchen, the aroma of tobacco led to a short hallway, then a softly lit room. As Chance stood there, the figure of a man appeared in the rectangle of light.

'Is that you Michael?'

Chance skirted the table and chairs in the middle of the room, pressed himself flat against the wall next to the hallway entrance.

As Luchese Senior entered, Chance pressed the gun softly against the side of his forehead. The old man didn't move.

'Is my boy okay?' he said.

'He might want to favour one arm for a while, but apart from that, he's alive. No more bullshit, he'll stay that way.'

The old man nodded. He wore an old plaid dressing gown over a white shirt, brown slacks and slippers. His jowls were covered with white stubble, the same colour as the whisps of hair pasted across his bald head.

'Your man, Angellini, he wasn't so lucky.'

Luchese gave an almost imperceptible shrug. Chance marvelled at the balls on the old guy. Cool as, like someone pulled a gun on him every day.

'Now we talk. You tell me what I want to know. You get your son back, safe and sound, and you never see me again. Do you understand?

'Yes.'

Chance followed Luchese up the hallway, past a set of stairs and into a wood-panelled living room. The old man lowered himself onto a beige leather couch, reached for a cigar, smouldering in an ashtray on a table, next to an empty tumbler and a mobile phone.

'That was stupid business, having my son pick you up and take you to the yard,' said Luchese in between pulling on the cigar, his voice a low growl.

Chance watched the old man readjusting to the new situation, a sharp mind in his old suit of skin.

'It was Michael's suggestion. He was worried, trying to protect me. My mistake. I should have taken you at your word.'

A brand-new flat screen television stood out amongst the otherwise old school décor: an oil painting of a gondola, a couple of easy chairs, a polished sideboard holding an assortment of framed photos. Chance picked one up, a young man, standing ramrod straight in military uniform,

'My brother's boy, Tony.' The embers at the end of Luchese's cigar fired into life as he puffed on it. 'He wasn't in the life. Joined the Marines. Died when he stepped on a mine in Iraq.'

Chance stared at the soldier's clean-cut features. He hardly looked out of his teens.

'Did you ever see service?' Luchese asked.

'One tour in East Timor, another in Afghanistan.'

'I know a few people who were in Afghanistan. It sounded bad.'

'I just drove trucks, did my best to avoid the rough stuff.' Saved that for my civilian life, thought Chance, putting the picture back on the sideboard.

'I had an uncle, drove trucks in France during World War II.'

Chance didn't have the time or interest in building rapport with the old man. He moved one of the easy chairs in front of Luchese, sat, held the pistol in his lap.

'What happened to your hand?'

Blood had started to spot the bandage on his wounded hand.

'Your man, Angellini, before I shot him.'

Luchese blinked, his eyes magnified by thick-rimmed glasses and topped by bushy eyebrows that ran in an almost unbroken line across his forehead.

'He was a good man, a good soldier. He knew the risks.'

'Just like Tony, yeah?'

A shadow passed over the old man's face. He was not used to being disrespected. He puffed on his cigar, releasing a plume of smoke into the air.

Chance took the photocopied newspaper picture of Luchese getting out of the car outside his trial for the Sonny Rosata slaying, unfolded it, and placed it on the coffee table between them.

'I want you to look at this carefully.' Chance tapped a finger on George Mundy's face. 'This man here is George Mundy. I assume he worked for you as a driver or bodyguard, I don't know. I want you to tell me everything you can remember about him. Leave nothing at all out. When I'm satisfied you have told me everything you know, I'll leave you in peace.'

'That was not his name when I knew him.' Luchese's face broke into a crooked half smile as he scanned the image. 'An associate in New York asked me whether I would mind looking after someone, an Australian, who needed to disappear for a while. It was a strange request, but it was a strange time. And my associate was not someone you ever said no to without a very good reason.'

Chance nodded for Luchese to continue.

'It was near the end of Little Nicky Scarfo's time. Scarfo was a greedy sonofabitch. Not content with labour unions and gambling, our traditional earners, he moved into drugs. Methamphetamines mainly, but also smack. Anyway, you go to bed with dogs, you get fleas. The drug business attracted all kinds of weirdos. I assumed this man, Mundy you call him, was one of them.'

Luchese puffed on his cigar in between sentences.

'Drugs were a good earner, but things got rather untidy.

Before Scarfo, someone stepped out of line, you dealt with it quietly. But Little Nicky liked problems to be solved as publicly as possible, as a warning to anyone else who was thinking of making trouble. I mean, I was used to rough stuff, but things were starting to get out of hand, even by my standards. Everyone was tense, always worried about getting whacked by Scarfo or a competitor, or being busted by the cops. Or the Feds.'

'You were asked to look after Mundy.' Chance pushed the conversation back on track. 'What happened then?'

'He drove for me for a while. I never trusted him, mainly on account of him being an outsider, not a *paisan*. But there was something else about him I didn't like.'

Chance waited as Luchese tapped the ash from his cigar.

'There were rumours Mundy was involved in a big heist in Australia, that he'd stiffed his partners on the take. It hardly made him Robinson Crusoe in the circles I moved in. But there was something else about him. It's hard to put into words, but the guy had a strange aura around him.'

'Strange how?'

'I know he had a sideline involved with smack while he was driving for me and didn't kick nothing back. Not that I could do anything about that on account of him being protected by New York. But it was his other interests that worried me more.'

'What other interests?'

'Agency business.'

'I don't understand.'

'The Central Intelligence Agency. There were rumours he'd worked with them in Vietnam, freelanced for them on and off since then.'

'You saying Mundy was a CIA spy.'

'I ain't saying nothing, and he certainly never did. Just telling you what I heard. Although it goes some way to explaining why he had influential friends.'

Luchese mashed the remains of his cigar in the ashtray,

scratched his crotch.

'Look kid, there were a lot of guys walking around after Vietnam, said they'd done all sorts of bad shit in that war. Some of them were full of it. Others were the real deal. It was kind of hard to sort out the shit from the Shinola, you catch my drift? Let's just say Mundy felt like the real deal.'

'My point being, an Australian with a face like a side of beef—no offence—suddenly appears in town, starts asking questions about someone from the bad old days I ain't seen for a long time. It rings alarm bells. Men in my line of business have long memories, and I didn't get to be old by being careless.'

Chance mulled over what the old man had told him, added it to what he knew about George Mundy: soldier, conman, armed robber, fence, spy. Mundy was like one of those magic eye pictures that wouldn't reveal its pattern, no matter how much you stared at it.

'We finished here?' The old man started to sit up.

'No. What happened to Mundy?'

Luchese's eyes hardened. He leaned back on the couch, his arms folded. 'Not until I see my son.'

Chance thought about what he'd heard about the cold-blooded way Luchese had killed his predecessor in the roofer's union and Christ only knew how many others. He'd met a few people like Luchese before, individuals capable of inflicting the most horrific violence one moment and cooing over a child the next.

Anger boiled up in Chance at having to humour the old man's pretence of being a dignified old school gangster any longer. He leapt up from the chair, kicked the coffee table hard, sending it and its contents flying across the room.

'You can save the wise guy shitfuckery for your get togethers at the social club,' Chance shouted. 'You kick loose with what you know or, so help me, I'll call my associates who are looking after your boy, tell them to add his body to the car compactor we fed Angellini into.'

Chance withdrew the burner from his jacket pocket for effect.

The old man's lips pursed, and his eyes narrowed in a poison-ous stare.

'I'll do better than tell you what happened to him. I'll show you where he is.'

Luchese sat in the back of the car with Chance, ignoring Jez except to give her a series of curt driving instructions. They cleared Philadelphia, the countryside becoming more rural, housing estates, stretches of forest and empty, well-tended paddocks.

At the outskirts of a medium-sized town, Luchese instructed Jez to turn into a stretch of road which ran through a heavily wooded area, emerging into a deserted car park surrounded by a U-shaped collection of shops, including a large supermarket, a hardware barn and an all-night pharmacy, its interior brilliant under white lights.

Without any introduction, Luchese started talking.

'The man you call George Mundy had been banging the wife of one of Scarfo's lieutenants,' he said without emotion. 'Word got out and, one night, the lieutenant and a couple of members from his crew were waiting for him as he left a bar. They dragged him into an alleyway and beat him half to death with tyre irons.

'Then they put him in a trunk, drove him here. It was all forest then. Way I heard it, they set fire to him while he was still alive and buried the remains,' Luchese looked out his window. 'If I'm not mistaken, under that hardware barn. First I knew about it was a phone call in the middle of the night from Little Nicky himself, telling me to find a new driver. To be honest, I was happy to see the back of the prick, although I got a lot of grief from my friends in New York.'

Chance picked over what he had been told for other leads.

'What about the guy whose wife he was fucking?'

'Died in jail ten years ago. Cancer. Don't know the names of the others involved.'

'And the wife.'

'Also dead.'

The old man sat up straight, his mouth set in a determined angle. 'Now make the fucking call, and let Michael go.'

Chance suddenly wanted to be as far away from Luchese as possible. He got out of the car, leaned against the bonnet, rolled a cigarette. He watched the first pink glow of dawn in the east as he smoked. The nicotine pushed up against a wave of exhausting washing over him.

'"The past is never dead",' said Jez, standing next to him. '"It's not even the past".'

'What?'

'Something a novelist once said.' Jez leaned against the bonnet, joined him in watching the dawn for a moment. 'Do I make the call to Kyrone and Jeff to let the son go?'

'Yeah.'

Chance's hand where the garrot had cut him hurt, and the back of his neck ached. He was too tired and ragged to be angry. He glanced over his shoulder at the old man. The car's overhead light gave Luchese's face a deathly pallor. He looked like a pensioner waiting to be driven to his local bingo game, instead of what he was, a bad man from a bad time.

ORPHAN ROAD

ORPHAN ROAD

ONE

Eva McCulloch got up from her laptop, stretched. She looked around the room in Leigh's apartment building that had been her home for the week since Chance had flown to the United States.

It had been his idea for her to move into Vera Leigh's while he was away. 'Easier and safer' was how he'd justified it.

'Safe from who?' she shot back.

'The police, for a start. Or have you forgotten the little case of arson and murder we were involved in only a few days ago?'

She had to admit he had a point.

Leigh's apartment complex was five storeys of architectural chaos, stairwells that led nowhere, rooms of various shapes and sizes, crammed with old, mismatched furniture and the detritus of Leigh's life. The place had obviously been intermittently renovated, but without any overall plan, to the point where it reminded Eva of the pencil drawing by that artist Escher of stairs that led into each other.

But the most fascinating feature was the photographs that plastered nearly every inch of wall space of Leigh hobnobbing with the rich and famous all over the world. Eva's favourite was a framed black-and-white photograph that had pride of place in a large oak panelled room on the ground floor: a visibly drunk and much younger Leigh dangling off the Rolling Stone's front man, Mick Jagger at a party in what looked like the seventies.

Eva had had a lot of time to think while Chance was away.

One of the things on her mind was whether she'd made the correct choice getting involved with him. The sex was convenient and good. Nothing wrong with that. She also liked his absolute lack of guile. What you saw was what you got. And while she'd given Chance a hard time about the whole going for one last big score before getting out of the life thing, if she were honest, she was no different.

Everyone has a version of the person they'd like to be and who they really are. Some people spend all their lives never realising the former. Eva liked to pride herself on letting as little daylight as possible between the two. She was a year shy of forty, an aging woman with pronounced criminal leanings and few marketable skills. Twenty years of long and short cons behind her, she had the smarts to realise her luck was running out. A few more years she'd be an old woman living in a car, dodging the police so she could wash in public toilet blocks. She needed money as much as Chance did. Perhaps more. As outlandish as the search for Mundy and the lost diamonds seemed, she had no option but to pursue it.

The wall above the desk in her room was plastered with handwritten notes and printouts from her research on George Mundy. In the centre of the mess of paper were the few existing photographs of him: Mundy standing next to the jeep in South Vietnam; in a Manila girlie bar; holding the car door open for a Philadelphian gangster in the late 1980s; and lastly, a family photograph that Sylvia had given her. Mundy celebrating Christmas in 1971, his first in Melbourne after coming back from Vietnam. He was wearing a paper crown, like the ones Eva remembered getting in Christmas crackers when she was a child. His face was angled away from the camera towards a barbecue.

Eva stared at the images, trying to connect the dots. The only pattern she'd managed to discern was that all the images had an accidental quality. Mundy had either been caught unawares, or in the case of the picture in which he was holding the car door open for the gangster, probably didn't even know he was being photographed. It fitted the general pattern of Mundy's life, a man who moved through the years trying to leave as little trace of his presence as possible.

Chance had asked her to find out as much about Mundy as she could while he was away. His request reeked of a bullshit assignment to keep her busy, but she tried to treat it seriously.

She was no Julian Assange, but neither was she a novice when it came to the internet and what you might learn from it. As far as Mundy was concerned, that was not a lot: a birth certificate proving he'd been born George Bartholomew Mundy in a town on the New South Wales side of the Murray River in 1944; death certificates for both parents.

His military file was classified, unsurprising given he had likely worked for army intelligence in Vietnam. The years following his return to civilian life were completely blank until his alleged involvement in the Bookie Robbery.

The internet was full of details about the robbery, the biggest Melbourne had ever seen, the sheer bloody audacity of it. This was followed by accounts of the usual heist gone wrong bullshit. The criminals had fallen out amongst themselves over ego and money. One by one, killed or missing.

And somewhere amongst the details Sylvia Mundy's contention was buried: that her father had been brought in to help launder a fortune in uncut diamonds that were part of the take but never reported to authorities.

Despite how things had gone wrong, Eva admired the men behind the heist, the patient and precise way they'd gone about planning and executing it. Not like her father, a junkie armed robber who'd spent most of the eighties knocking over bank branches and building societies in Perth's outer suburbs. Places with minimal if any security and no guards, a couple of bank tellers, usually young women, whom he and his partner would threaten with sawn offs for the contents of the cash drawers, most of the pre-job planning having taken place the day before.

Her father used to boast that he was able to get in and out of any bank he robbed in under a minute, flush with cash. That either went up his arm or was pissed away on booze. Days in a row where Eva was left with her father's friends and relatives while he partied after a job, her mother long gone from the scene.

It wasn't much of a childhood, but it had its moments, mainly the times the two of them went camping. Long days spent exploring Western Australia's dry red deserts. Nights sleeping on swags out in the open. He would keep her entertained with what she suspected were largely made up takes about his life and play guitar to her.

It went on like this until the day her father got careless, did a job while loaded on cheap speed, accidentally shot and killed a teller who'd been putting cash into a bag too slowly. Eva remembered a brief, heavily publicised manhunt, which ended with the police tracking Liam McCulloch down and arresting him in a caravan park south of Bunbury.

Her father claimed the shotgun had gone off accidentally. The jury took less than an hour to return a unanimous verdict of guilty, and her father went to prison for the rest of his life. Eva recalled the story plastered across the front page of the city's papers, along with her father's mugshot, his mop of thick black hair, lopsided grin, and beady eyes.

Among the skills her father had taught her was how to make a good campfire, how to drive, and how to use a knife. She liked to joke that his criminal tendencies had inspired her brief time in real estate. They were also a formative influence on another childhood habit she developed: she liked to break into and prowl unoccupied houses. She never took anything, didn't even touch stuff most of the time. She just got off on the illicit thrill of being where she shouldn't, pretending she was a bank robber like her father, casing a potential job.

As for her knife skills, she'd first used those on an uncle she been sent to live with after her father had been jailed. The uncle had tried to crawl into bed with her and got a steak knife that Eva had smuggled from the kitchen in his thigh for his trouble.

She'd ended up a ward of the state but got lucky when, a year later, the system spat her out into the care of a couple, Maggie, a librarian, and her husband, Rory.

Maggie made Eva read, and Rory introduced her to computers.

Rory, whose wild head of frizzy dark hair and bushy beard reminded her of the poet Allen Ginsberg, had been a prominent student activist at university and an early adopter of computer technology. Rory sold his services to a couple of private investigators, unearthing hard to find information, and spent most of his time in his home office, tapping away on various keyboards, surrounded by shelves filled with files and a jungle of wires, cords and pieces of equipment.

It was thanks to Rory's tutelage Eva could grasp how hard it was to move through life leaving no trail, even in pre-internet times, as George Mundy had done. As a long-term undertaking, it involved discipline, high-level knowledge, and serious resources.

The only mention of Mundy she found in the online media was in a newspaper colour piece written to mark the passing of Brian Grove, the owner of the Manila bar who had supposedly played host to Mundy for several months after he'd fled Melbourne.

Grove's establishment, or "Asian vice den," as the article referred to it, allegedly functioned as a stop-over for escapees and crooks on their way out of Australia, and a meeting place for drug runners and arms dealers. That is until the Philippines dictatorship which had been providing Grove with protection was overthrown in 1986, and he was deported to Australia, where he spent his remaining days in relative obscurity and poverty.

Similar details had been regurgitated by the veritable cottage industry of true crime blogs and podcasts on the internet. Eva trawled through these and the plethora of websites and blogs operated by expatriates in the Philippines, most of them little more than guides to the cheapest local sex for sale. Badly written and laid out, they were plastered with pictures of bored looking Filipinas pole dancing and propping up bars wearing nothing but skimpy bikinis and high heels, next to overweight white men.

There were one or two mentions of Grove's bar, Brown Honey. Located in the heart of the Philippines capital's red-light district, Makati, it was much missed by Manila's few surviving long-term expats and newer arrivals wanting a taste of the city in its more wicked and lawless days. But none of the sites made any mention of Mundy.

After she'd exhausted her online inquiries, Eva spent time in the State Library consulting books on Australian army intelligence activities in Vietnam. Mundy scored a brief mention in a long out of print autobiography by a former Australian soldier, now dead, as a member of an elite unit known by the innocuous title of 'the Australian Army Training Team'. Dispatched to Saigon two years before Australia officially entered the war in 1965, according to the book, several of the Team were assigned to assist Central Intelligence Agency operations against the Viet Cong. It was real Colonel Kurtz stuff: Australian spooks working with ethnic minority tribesmen deep in the jungles of central Vietnam. Some members were even rumoured to have taken part in a covert Agency assassination activity known as the Phoenix Program.

All up, not much to show for a week's work, Eva thought as she watched the setting sun cast a shadow across her desk. She stood in front of the window, surveyed the rooftops surrounding Leigh's apartment complex. The silhouette of a large construction crane loomed several blocks away, one of a dozen or so that dotted Melbourne's skyline. She hugged herself against a sudden chill. It had been several days since she'd last heard from Chance, and she missed him. Mostly for the way he acted as a buffer between her and the others.

Eva felt Leigh's disapproval and she neither liked nor trusted the older woman.

She been given a room on the fourth storey of Leigh's apartment complex, one floor below that occupied by Vera. Eva hadn't ventured upstairs since she and Chance had last been there together to discuss the job, and the only conversation they'd exchanged was when Leigh had informed her Ruth Mundy had died.

Then there was Leigh's silent slab of a bodyguard, Angel, who always looked at her with suspicion and had hardly said a complete sentence to her the entire time she'd been here.

If Eva needed anything, she went directly to Loomis. He'd arranged the computer equipment, other stuff she wanted. She liked the old man and could tell, from the way his eyes beamed at her whenever they spoke, it was reciprocated. There was the faint trace of an English accent in Loomis's voice and an agile mind underneath the shambolic exterior. But like Leigh, he remained a mystery.

In between her research on Mundy, Eva devoted time to looking into her host's past. Vera had been a regular feature in the social pages of Melbourne's newspapers in the eighties and nineties. Race meets, balls, sporting grand finals, fashion events. Rich people loved a touch of the illicit and "Melbourne's naughty madam", as Leigh was often described, provided it in spades.

The mentions got fewer as public tastes changed and Melbourne slowly gentrified, drying up almost completely as the city moved into the new century. The one exception, a relatively recent newspaper article about a large property developer attempting to buy and redevelop a seedy part of Melbourne. The company had slowly purchased one property after another until all that was left was Leigh's S&M dungeon.

A company spokesperson talked up their campaign to clean up the city's sleaze. Leigh shot back with accusations of shadowy overseas interests, putting the squeeze on a long-standing local business. The article discussed her controversial past and declining business fortunes. There was a colour picture, clearly taken in one of the rooms of her establishment. Leigh, wearing a leopard skin-body suit and matching turban, posed next to a shelf of mannequin heads fitted with various wigs, the wall behind her covered in vivid red flocked wallpaper. Her best quote: "I've had judges, politicians, captains of industry, and even the odd TV news weatherman walk through the doors of my establishment. So don't talk to me about morality."

Eva switched off her laptop and put on a hoodie against the cold. She was zipping up the front, deliberating what to do with her night, when the power went off.

TWO

Eva sat on her narrow bed, darkness closing in around her. Eventually she noticed the shaft of pale light from the window, the noise of the city outside. She pressed her face against the pane of glass. The streets around Leigh's apartment thrummed with early evening activity and the lights were on in the windows of the nearby offices.

Nowhere else had been affected by the blackout. It was only Leigh's building which had no power.

Eva opened the door to her room, peered into the hallway that connected it with the rest of the complex, just in time to see Loomis approaching her from the other direction. Stooping slightly, he held a hurricane lamp above his head and in his rumpled black suit, white shirt and bright red cravat, looked like he'd just stepped out of one of the gothic mysteries favoured by her late foster mother.

'Are you aware it's just this building that appears to have no power?' Eva said.

'Yes, Miss McCulloch, that fact has not escaped me.' Loomis paused, waited for Eva to reach him, then turned and started walking back from where he'd come.

'Your boss late with paying the power bill or something?'

'No.' Loomis started to descend a narrow set of wooden stairs.

'Then don't you think it's strange?'

'Highly. I fear we might have unwelcome visitors.' He turned to her, the flame from the swaying lantern dancing in his large, dark eyes. 'I don't suppose it would make any difference if I asked you to stay in your room until the matter is sorted?'

'None whatsoever.'

'I didn't think so.' Loomis nodded. 'In that case, follow me and please be careful.'

Loomis turned left at the bottom of the stairs, made his way along a piece of frayed Persian carpet lining a narrow hallway which ended in another stairwell, its entrance flanked by rusting suits of armour.

Despite prowling the house many times over the last week, Leigh's bizarre domicile remained as much of a mystery to Eva as ever. 'Where are we going?'

'To meet up with Angel. I've sent him ahead to check the main electrical panel. It's in an alcove behind the kitchen.'

Loomis's breath became slightly laboured as he descended the stairs. 'I really must see to getting the service elevator fixed when all this is over.'

'You can start by putting doors on it for a start,' said Eva. 'That open shaft is a serious hazard. Then again, why stop with just the elevator? With the money from her share of the diamonds, Leigh could redecorate, completely change up the creepy haunted house vibe she's got going.'

'It grows on you after a while.'

'Yeah, like a fungus.' Eva sniggered. 'And where is the mistress of the house?'

'Upstairs in her room. She proved more open to my suggestion to stay put than you.'

'You mean she's drunk again.'

'We all have our vices, Ms McCulloch. You should have seen her back in the day. She was a force to be reckoned with.'

'I'll take your word for it.'

At the bottom of the stairs, Loomis stopped, swung the lantern in a hundred-and-eighty-degree arc. The illumination showed a large oak panelled room, the wooden floor covered in a square of faded red carpet, leather armchairs and sofas arranged around the room, a large fireplace, a mound of ashes from its last blaze.

'Please wait here a moment.' Loomis disappeared through a doorway that led to the building's entrance. Eva thought about following him, but worried she might get lost in the dark, did as she was told. She wished she had a better handle on the layout. Most of all, she wished she had a weapon.

Loomis reappeared a few moments later.

'Where the hell did you go?' she hissed.

'To check the front door. It's locked.'

'Which means what?'

'If there's someone in the house, they didn't get in that way.'

Loomis gestured to a darkened doorway that led to the kitchen.

'Angel,' Loomis called softly, then repeated it slightly louder.

No response, but Eva was sure she heard something moving about in the kitchen.

Loomis heard it too, froze.

'Rats?' Whispered Eva.

'Yes, of the two-legged variety.'

With his free hand, Loomis reached inside his suit jacket and withdrew a pistol. In one of those useless pieces of information the mind files away, Eva recognised the bulky piece of metal from all the war films she'd watched with her father as a child, a German Luger.

'Miss McCulloch, you really would be safer if you had stayed in your room,' Loomis hissed.

'Too late for that now.'

Loomis emitted a world-weary sigh. 'Oh well, into the Valley of Death rode the six hundred.' Loomis stepped into the kitchen, holding the lantern in front of him. It revealed two large benches, an industrial fridge and oven. Eva could vaguely make out the deep blackness of the disused lift shaft to her right. A cold room and a walk-in pantry to the left. In the middle, the alcove that held the electrical board.

She followed Loomis, pausing next to the first bench. On it sat a knife block. She quietly slid a medium-sized knife out of the holder, held it at her side. If Loomis noticed, he said nothing, momentarily disappearing into the alcove.

'Well, that explains the blackout,' he called out. 'Someone has cut the circuits.'

Emboldened by the knife in her hand, Eva stepped towards the pantry. She had only taken a few steps when the surface beneath her somehow lost its grip. She felt herself slip, grunted as she fell to the ground.

Loomis crouched down next to her, holding the lantern over his head. 'Are you alright—' His question trailed off.

She followed his gaze, recoiled as she recognised Angel's body lying next to her. Dark liquid seeped from the jagged wound that had once been the right side of his forehead. His Ray Bans lay in the pool of blood that ballooned around him, revealing eyes staring lifelessly at the ceiling.

Eva backed away until she pressed up against the leg of one of the kitchen benches. One of her hands felt wet. She raised it in front of her, saw it was covered with Angel's blood.

She breathed deeply, unsure what to do, waited for Loomis to say something.

His possum eyes flickered, broke away from Angel. 'Vera,' he said, almost to himself. 'She's in danger.'

As Loomis turned to leave, Eva saw a figure emerge from the gloom behind him, a flash of something metallic and the old man fell to the ground. The pistol clattered into the darkness and the lantern fell onto the floor, hissed as it shattered and was extinguished in Angel's blood. The room was thrown into darkness.

Eva could make out the shape of someone moving towards her. Remembering the knife, she raised it, slashed the blade back and forth several times in front of her. She felt the blade bite into something on one of her swings. An unfamiliar male voice cursed.

Not wanting to step in the spreading pool of Angel's blood and end up back on her arse again, she felt for the bench. She found it, steadied herself against it with her free hand, and swung her body on top and over to the other side.

As Eva moved into the centre of the kitchen, she felt her attacker close behind.

'Fucking little bitch,' he spat.

She gripped the knife hilt hard, wielded it in a combination of jabs and slashes in the direction of the voice, but failed to make contact. She jabbed again, felt the blade clang against a heavier piece of metal. The impact sent the knife spinning out of her hand.

Her assailant pressed his advantage, came at her swinging the piece of metal in his hands. Eva, aware of the object cutting the air right in front of her face, backed away, until the floor suddenly disappeared beneath her. A brief, violent fall, broken only by one of her hands managing to cling to the edge of the empty elevator shaft.

The wind knocked from her, Eva dangled for a moment, her legs kicking against the empty darkness. She heard Loomis moan and her attacker pause for breath, knew the only way she would survive was to make him think she had fallen to the bottom of the shaft and his job was done.

She tried to steady herself against the wall of the shaft, took a deep breath, held it as the man approached the edge. He stood there, cleared his throat, spat into the shaft. The phlegm caught her on the forehead, and she had to steel herself from reacting in disgust as the thick spittle oozed down her cheek. She heard the man turn and leave.

When she thought he was out of earshot, Eva reached her other arm up and gripped the edge of the lift shaft with both hands. The rough concrete tore against her shoulders and breasts as she tried to simultaneously lift herself out and swing her legs up onto the floor. She managed to get both elbows and the top half of her body over the edge, but failed to completely pull herself out.

She felt herself getting weaker, the knowledge she couldn't hold on for much longer, that she probably only had the strength for one attempt seeped through her, made her feel heavier. Eva was about to try once more when she heard footsteps approach, saw a light, terrified her attacker was returning to double check she had not survived.

Eva took a deep breath, stopped moving and tried to make herself as small as possible. But her arms and head were visible to anyone who came close enough. She was completely defenceless.

The figure was indistinct behind a small handheld light, but their outline appeared heavier than her previous attacker. Maybe there was more than one of them. The figure crouched down next to Loomis for a moment, moved the light over the prone figure, then shone it directly into Eva's face.

'What are you waiting for, fuckhead?' she slurred, squinting against the light. 'Get it over with.'

The figure ran over, reached down and before she could react, gripped one of her forearms, pulled and suddenly she was out of the shaft.

Eva sat up. Her breath escaped in ragged gasps. She was too exhausted to resist any further.

'I leave you people alone for a week and everything goes to shit.'

She did a double take, unsure if she had heard the voice correctly. As he knelt next to her, Chance's identikit face came into view.

'That makes us even for you saving my skin at the commune.' He smiled. 'By the way, you look like shit, mate.'

She noticed his bandaged hand, smiled. 'You don't look so crash hot yourself.' She leant up to kiss him, pushed hard against his lips, prised his teeth apart with her tongue, savoured the mixture of nicotine and his unique taste, not wanting to stop.

Loomis groaned. She broke away, glanced in his direction.

'He'll have a nasty bump, but I think he's okay,' Chance replied to her unanswered question. 'Angel's not so lucky,' he said as he cradled her head against his chest.

'Why didn't you call or email, let us know you were coming back?'

'It's a long story. Let's just say what happened in America made me a little paranoid about my movements.'

Her clothes were streaked with dirt and sweat. She kneaded the muscles in her hands. The top half of her body arched from the strain of holding onto the edge of the lift shaft and trying to pull herself up.

'What the hell happened here?' said Chance.

'What does it look like, genius? We were attacked.'

'Who by?'

'I don't know.' Eva grunted in pain as she slowly stood up. Every muscle in her body was sore. 'Why don't you ask your friend and his employer, Leigh? I've got a feeling she might know.'

'I would if I could find her.'

'What do you mean?'

'Leigh's not in her apartment. She's disappeared.'

THREE

Chance made the last repairs to the power board of Leigh's apartment complex. It was obvious whoever had disabled it hadn't known what they were doing, attempting a crude smash job but doing minimal damage.

The power restored, Chance briefly paused next to the freshly scrubbed area of polished concrete floor where Angel's body, temporarily stashed in the cool room, had bled out.

It hadn't taken much to deduce the individuals who'd snatched Leigh had entered via the patio on the second floor, accessed without too much difficulty from the rooftop of the vacant adjoining building. A smashed pane of glass on one of the French doors was all it took. It was that simple.

Chance figured it for at least a two- or three-person job. One of the assailants entered first to disable the power board and was discovered by Angel. Once Angel was dealt with and the power was out, the others entered and grabbed Leigh.

The only thing unclear in Chance's mind was how they managed to navigate the rabbit warren of Leigh's apartment building so quickly and precisely. They must have had the layout of the place down pat, which suggested inside knowledge.

As attested by a smashed tumbler and an upended bottle of vodka, Leigh had put up a fight. Chance smiled grimly to himself as he imagined the kidnappers wrestling with the drunken, recalcitrant old woman, hoped that was the worst she'd have of it until he could find out who took her and how to get her back.

Chance sat down heavily in one of the chairs arranged around the coffee table, let himself sink into the sagging leather and rolled himself a cigarette. The room and its contents, the dusty mismatched furniture, the faded photographs on the walls, the disused screens and old telephones, the diorama of stuffed animals, all of it seemed even more pathetic and out of place in the world without its owner.

His eyes lingered on Leigh's well-stocked bar cart. He thought about pouring himself a drink but dismissed the idea until he had debriefed with Eva and Loomis. Ten p.m. Melbourne time was early morning in New York. His body clock was still on American time, though he was exhausted after the twenty-four-hour flight.

Eva sat in the chair next to him, legs tucked under her, sipped a glass of Leigh's single malt, the bottle and her unopened laptop on the table in front of her. Freshly showered, her black hair still damp and spiky, she wore a lime green silk dressing gown, one of the many Leigh owned.

'You okay?'

She smiled, nodded slightly, the strain of the day's events still etched on her features. Chance wondered whether she was in shock.

Loomis lay stretched out on the long brown leather couch opposite them. His bloodstained shirt and jacket lay in a heap on the floor, and he wore only his suit trousers and a grimy white singlet.'

The pale skin on his scrawny chest and arms looked like it had never seen the sun's rays. He held a large joint in one hand and an icepack to his head in the other. His Luger and a large cut glass ashtray sat on the table next to him.

'Poor Angel, he was a good friend and comrade.' Loomis puffed hard on the joint, held the smoke for a moment and then blew it into the air above him. 'He deserved better than to be bludgeoned to death by some anonymous ne'er-do-well and stuck in a cooler.

'"His life was gentle; and the elements so mixed in him, that nature might stand up and to all the world. This was a man!"' Loomis's voice rose as he spoke. 'That's Shakespeare's *Julius Caesar* for the benefit of you ignorant heathens.'

There's not much dignity in lying in a food freezer, Chance agreed with that much, but it was not as though they could go to the police. Having witnessed the force Leigh's former bodyguard had used to eject unwanted guests from her parties, however, gentle was not a word Chance would never have associated with the dead man.

'Just count yourself lucky, Loomis, whoever hit you was a bad aim, otherwise we'd have to dispose of two corpses,' Chance said. 'You sure you don't need a doctor?'

'I've had worse, Gary. Anti-Vietnam War rally in London's Grosvenor Square, March 1968.' Loomis pulled hard on the joint, stared at the ceiling, as he relived the moment. 'Eight thousand of us were charged by the blue bottles. One of the fascist pigs pulled me by the hair, while a couple of others liberally administered some law and order with their truncheons. I got a night in the West End police station and sympathy sex from the daughter of a prominent Tory politician who was in the same cell for my troubles.'

Chance picked up a metal lighter from the table in the shape of a mermaid, fired up his cigarette, as he exchanged eye rolls with Eva.

'Not something I expect someone with your military history to appreciate,' added Loomis, pointedly.

Chance let the crack go through to the keeper, looked at his watch.

'If it is not too much trouble, can we cut to it?'

Eva killed her drink. 'Why don't you start by telling us what happened in America?'

Eva and Loomis were silent as Chance ran down the main points.

'And that bandaged hand is courtesy of one of the people

reluctant to talk about Mundy?' Eva asked when Chance had finished.

Chance nodded.

'Does it still hurt?'

'Yes.'

'So, the upshot is Mundy is dead?' said Loomis.

'It would appear so,' said Chance.

'What that gangster, Luchese said about Mundy maybe being a spy, it chimes with the little I managed to find out about his activities in Vietnam.'

Chance raised an eyebrow inquisitively. Eva took it as a sign, filled her companions in on what she had discovered over the last few days.

Loomis sat up, the smouldering joint poised in front of his face. 'A maybe not so ex-spy, ninety million in lost diamonds, shady organised crime figures, the plot doth thicken, wouldn't you say?'

'Possibly,' said Chance. 'Or, the whole story is, and has always been, complete and utter bullshit.'

Loomis gave a non-committal shrug.

'There are other possibilities,' Eva said.

Chance rubbed his bandaged hand. 'Such as?'

'That there are details about her father's life Sylvia Mundy has been a little reticent to share with us. Or Leigh might not have briefed us on all the information she had.'

'This is a question we can easily ask the daughter,' said Chance. 'And Leigh...once we find her.'

'Which brings us to the question of who might have taken her.' Eva eyed Loomis. 'Her line of business, she must have had enemies.'

'Do I detect a note of censure in your question, Miss McCulloch? Granted, it may not seem like it in these increasingly puritanical times, but running an S&M dungeon is like any other business only, if anything, the clientele runs to the more financially well-heeled end of the spectrum, even if these people are keen not to advertise their patronage.'

Loomis readjusted the icepack on his head as he spoke.

'And it is true, Vera has also had her share of run ins with Melbourne's criminal class, in and out of uniform. But there is still an honour among thieves, so to speak. If we are looking for suspects in her disappearance, can I suggest her recent business problems may offer a more fruitful avenue of investigation?'

'Are you suggesting the developer who was leaning on Leigh to sell up is responsible for her disappearance?'

'That is exactly what I am suggesting.' Loomis continued, mashing out the remains of his joint for emphasis.

Eva poured herself another finger from the bottle of single malt on the table. 'How serious was Leigh's fight with these people?'

'For a long time, not so serious.' Loomis grinned, exposing a row of crooked yellow teeth. 'She relished being a thorn in the side of their attempts to clean up the so-called seedy stretch of town. The publicity it generated even gave business a bit of a boost for a while.

'But over the last few months, things got nasty, especially as the developer bought out more of the street and Leigh's establishment was the last holdout. Long-term customers were lent on to stop coming, suppliers suddenly ceased delivering. There was even pressure from the city council to sell.'

'I remember Vera telling me someone was after her, that she felt unsafe,' Chance said. 'But from leaning on a few customers to kidnapping and murder is a pretty major escalation.'

'Maybe, or business by other means,' Loomis said firmly. 'Leigh's refusal to budge was holding up their redevelopment plans. And that was costing them serious money.'

Eva, who had opened her laptop and been typing away while the two men spoke, looked up. 'White Cube Property Investment,' she said.

'What are you talking about?' said Chance, irritated.

'That's the name of the business trying to buy out Leigh. I

read about them in a newspaper article. Let's see what else there is about them on the internet.' She turned back to the screen. 'A stylish but uninformative website. Lists the managing director as a Warwick Hamilton.'

Loomis proceeded to fix himself another joint from a half empty plastic bag of marijuana on the coffee table. Chance sat back, watched Eva, her brow furrowed in concentration as she continued to type on her keyboard.

"I'll do a deeper search later but at first glance, Hamilton is a man who likes to keep to himself,' she said several minutes later. 'But there is this, an article in a business magazine from a couple of years ago about who's who in terms of property ownership in the beachside Melbourne suburb of Portsea. "Australia's richest postcode, where old traditions and new money meet",' she read aloud.

'And this is where Mister Hamilton calls home.' Eva recited an address as she swivelled the screen around to reveal a colour photograph of a modern double storey dwelling on a clifftop overlooking a beach. Wooden stairs wound their way down from the property through thick foliage to a beach box and private jetty, extending out into the turquoise water.

Eva smiled at Chance. 'One thing I learnt during my brief time in real estate, it is that while the rich might like their privacy, what they like even more is to let other people know they're rich.'

'I think it is time we pay Mister Hamilton a visit.' Loomis's face broke into an impish grin.

'What do you mean "we"?' said Chance.

'I will of course be accompanying you, Gary.'

Chance started to disagree but Loomis cut him off.

'When I first came to Melbourne in the eighties, I was a penniless alcoholic. Vera gave me a job and helped me get off the booze. I've been working in various capacities for her ever since. It has been one of the most painful things in my life, watching those posh bastards drive her business into the ground over the last few months, seeing her start to fall apart, coping with the stress through drinking and other means.'

Loomis lay his half-rolled joint on the table as he spoke.

'This is on top of what happened tonight. A grave security breach for which I hold myself solely responsible, which resulted in Angel's death and put my employer's life in mortal danger. As long as there's a possibility Vera is alive, I am going to help you get her back safely. Once that is accomplished, we can resume our search for the diamonds, or the both of you can fuck off. I shan't debate the matter further.'

He patted the Luger on the table, his big bloodshot eyes moving between his two companions until they nodded their agreement.

The old man smiled, resumed making his joint.

'Good, now if neither of you don't mind, I am going to smoke this spliff, then there's work to do.'

He looked around the room, spoke to no one in particular. '"Sound trumpets! Let our bloody colours wave! And either victory, or else a grave."'

FOUR

Eva parked next to the nature strip, got out of the car, sniffed. A vague shit smell drifted in from the nearby sewerage treatment works.

The three of them had agreed on a division of labour the previous night: she would track down Sylvia Mundy, while Loomis and Chance braced the managing director of White Cube Investment.

Eva had tried to contact Sylvia by phone all morning. She'd even rung the hospital pretending to be a distant friend of Ruth Mundy, wanting to get hold of Sylvia so she could express her condolences over her mother's death. The nurse on duty told Eva the last they'd seen of Sylvia was three days earlier, when she had come in to collect her mother's things.

Having decided there was nothing for it but to visit Sylvia in person, Eva descended to the underground garage with the keys Loomis had given her to Leigh's car. Eva whistled as she threw the tarp off the vehicle. An appreciation of muscle cars was another thing she'd inherited from her father, and she instantly recognised the make: a Ford XB GS Falcon, mustard coloured with a black racing stripe along the side.

'Not exactly low-key, but fuck it,' she said under her breath.

Eva took her time, enjoyed the way the Falcon handled, almost disappointed when she finally arrived at the address she had for Sylvia in Melbourne's far western suburbs.

The house was one in a row of near identical single-storey cream-brick and red corrugated iron-roofed dwellings separated by sagging timber fences, all sitting behind low brick front fences of the same colour. There was a garage on one side, the roller door down, a narrow path to the backyard on the other. The curtains on the front window were closed.

'What a shithole,' Eva muttered. It reminded her of the house in Perth she had lived as a child.

The front lawn was still brown from the blasting it had received over summer, but a lemon tree and a hedge of purple hydrangeas thrived. Eva opened a tiny front gate, walked up a path lined with white pebbles and several weather-beaten gnome statues, and knocked on the front door.

She waited a few moments, knocked again. Nothing.

She went down the side of the house, emerged into a backyard that felt like it belonged in the 1960s: a small, ramshackle shed, an ancient-looking Hills Hoist clothesline in the centre of another square of sun blasted grass.

The pair of thin lace curtains were partly drawn on the kitchen window. Eva peered inside, saw nothing out of place. She entered the garage through a rear door. An older model Holden Commodore sat in the otherwise empty space.

Eva spun the clothesline as she pondered her next steps. It creaked as it slowly circled.

Maybe her mother's death had sliced clean through the last ties anchoring Sylvia to her old life. Eva tried to imagine the woman hastily throwing clothes into a suitcase and getting the hell out of town while she had a few good years left. But if so, Sylvia would've needed wheels, and hers were still in the garage.

Eva was checking the mailbox, crammed with what looked like a few days' mail, when she felt herself being watched. She looked up, saw a youngish woman standing in next-door's front yard, a baby cradled in her arms.

Without missing a beat, Eva walked up to the fence separating the properties.

'Hi, hospital welfare, come to check on Sylvia,' she said, hoping the neighbour hadn't seen her pull up in the Ford XB GS Falcon, put two and two together and come up with the obvious conclusion Eva was lying.

'I was terribly sad to hear about Ruth's passing,' said the young woman. The infant squirmed in the woman's arms, and there were dark circles under her eyes.

'Yes, terrible news. But at least she is no longer suffering.'

The young woman flashed a wan smile, nodded as she repositioned the child on her hip.

'You wouldn't happen, by any chance, to know where Sylvia is?'

'Last I saw of her was a couple of nights ago. I was feeding this one here, and I saw her from my front window. She was getting into a car with two men. Haven't seen her since.'

'Any idea who the men were?'

The woman gave Eva a brief description of the men.

'It's none of my business, of course, but I thought she might be going out to have some fun. She deserves it after the year she's had.'

Eva nodded thanks. She pulled her mobile phone from the back pocket of her jeans as she walked towards the car and dialled Loomis's number.

FIVE

The three-seater fibreglass speedboat bobbed on the gentle ocean swell of Port Phillip Bay. The vessel had been hastily procured by Loomis, who piloted it with surprising skill. No doubt it helped the old man was straight. He'd assured Chance he wouldn't so much as smell a joint while they were working. As far as Chance could tell, Loomis had been true to his word.

Hamilton's cliff-top residence was visible about twenty metres away, its starkly designed modern angles etched against the night sky, one in a string of million-dollar properties, the lights from which dotted the westernmost tip of the Mornington Peninsula.

En route to the Peninsula, Loomis had diverted the boat to a deep channel in the bay, where they disposed of Angel.

'Two birds with one stone and all that,' said Loomis as he and Chance wrestled with the body, wrapped in canvas and weighed down with house bricks. 'I pierced his stomach to let the air out, so our friend should stay sunk.'

'Why do I think this is not the first time you've done this?'

Loomis didn't reply. He stood erect, as Angel's body disappeared into the dark water.

'"We therefore commit his body to the deep, to be turned into corruption",' intoned Loomis solemnly, '"looking for the resurrection of the body, when the sea shall give up her dead".'

At least Angel would have company. Chance thought grimly of Dormer, who'd stiffed Chance on his share of a heist they had committed and then tried to kill him. Chance had returned the favour by tying Dormer to an old bar fridge and pushing him off a boat into the depths of the same bay.

As Loomis restarted the boat to resume their journey, Chance wondered how many other bodies the bay held in secret.

Eva, parked within sight of the front driveway of the Hamilton residence, had phoned and given them the heads up when their target had arrived home just before sunset. Further research on Eva's part had established the real estate developer was a bachelor, but he had a female friend with him.

Several of the ground floor and first storey windows that faced the beach were softly lit. Watching from the boat, a tall man, Hamilton, and a blonde woman, were visible. No one else.

It struck Chance that if Hamilton had a hand in Leigh's disappearance, he'd have arranged additional security. But there was no sign of any such precautions.

His body clock still on American time, though Chance had slept much of the day, he still felt terrible, like he was coming down with a bad flu. More concerning was the gnawing feeling in his gut that kicked in whenever a job didn't feel right. And what he was about to do felt a long way from anything resembling smart or right.

First Leigh. And now, according to Eva, Sylvia Mundy was also missing. Chance didn't buy for a second the possibility, put forward by Eva, that Sylvia had simply gone AWOL as some sort of show of freedom now her mother was dead.

And while it was one thing to suggest Hamilton might've had a hand in Leigh's disappearance, the developer had nothing to gain by taking Sylvia Mundy as well. Something else was up. Chance knew it, but he couldn't put the pieces together.

'You ready, old boy?' Loomis said.

Chance wore a black T-shirt, black canvas pants, and a black windbreaker to ward off the early autumn chill. Slung across his back was a slim canvas bag with the tools he needed to get into Hamilton's.

He continued to watch the house as he slipped on black leather gloves, felt the weight of the Luger nestled between his jeans and the small of his back.

'You're sure this antique actually works?' Chance had asked when Loomis offered him the gun.

Loomis huffed. 'Taken off a dead Nazi officer at Normandy, or so the bloke who sold it to me said. A precision piece of engineering from the time when pistols were not the single use items they are today. It'll make a hell of a racket so only to be used as a last recourse.'

The two men had discussed the possibility of bracing Hamilton at his office, but discounted it as too public, with too many variables they couldn't control. His house made the most logical option.

The plan was for Loomis to drop Chance behind the rocky outcrop at the base of the cliff. Chance would enter the house, do whatever was necessary to find out where Leigh was, or eliminate the real estate developer as a suspect in her disappearance. And get out as quickly as possible.

It was a good, simple plan, utilising the only factor in their favour: surprise. Hamilton would not expect to be hit so quickly or so hard. But it was a rush job, Google Earth and whatever else Eva had found on the internet standing in for the more thorough casing out of the property. Chance felt the lack of preparation keenly as Loomis piloted the boat to within a few metres of the rocky outcrop. The old man handed Chance his last bit of equipment, a black cotton balaclava. 'Good luck,' he said.

Chance put it on, nodded, jumped into the freezing cold water, waded several steps towards the shore. He took a pair of canvas runners out of his bag, put them on and sprinted towards the wooden stairs leading up to the house. The stairs emerged onto a stretch of lawn, beyond which was a sandstone tiled patio in front of a set of sliding glass doors. A small camera unit was fixed to the wall on the left side of the doors.

Chance crouched in the darkness, scanned the area in front of him. The glass doors revealed a tastefully furnished room, with a long dining table and chairs, Aboriginal artwork on the walls. It was lit by a single lamp on a sideboard against one of the walls. The muffled sound of classical music emanated through the glass.

Chance skirted the stretch of lawn, crouched under the camera. He unslung the canvas bag, withdrew a spray can of black paint, reached up and sprayed until the lens was completely covered.

He tried the handle. Locked. He took out several instruments from the bag and laid them out in a row on the ground: a round piece of plastic, a permanent marker pen, a glass cutter, a small rock hammer, and an industrial suction cup same size as the round piece of plastic and capable of lifting five kilos.

He moved as fast as he could, his bandaged hand providing minimal interference with his movements. He placed the piece of plastic on the glass next to the latch that locked the door, traced around it with the marker. Then, with the glass cutter, he scored the circle several times, gave it one hard tap with the hammer. The glass within the circle splintered. Last, he attached the suction cup to the circular section of glass, pulled. The glass came away more or less in a neat circle.

Chance threw the equipment back in the canvas bag, re-slung it over his shoulder, reached in, undid the latch, and opened the door.

Taking out the Luger, he cocked it by pulling the toggle-lock, as Loomis had shown him, moved around the dining table, then followed the music up the stairs and into a lounge room, furnished with couches, a wet bar, and an ornate looking stereo system. A large fish tank against one wall bathed the room in soft blue light, tiny darts of colour visible in the water. To the right was a hallway, light emanating from the half-closed door at the end.

Chance heard female laughter, flattened himself against the wall to one side of the hallway. The sound of the door opening, soft footfalls and a woman emerged into the lounge room in a black silk dressing gown.

Before she could register his presence, Chance grabbed her from behind, put his hand hard on her mouth, jabbed the gun barrel into her side.

'Don't make a sound and I promise you won't get hurt,' said Chance calmly. 'Nod if you understand.'

The woman nodded, her eyes wide with terror.

Chance took his hand away from her mouth. 'What is your name?' he said in her ear, just loud enough to be heard above the music.

'Nicole,' she said hesitantly.

'Nicole, is there anyone else here besides you and Warwick?' Chance said, deliberately using first names to put her at ease.

She shook her head.

'I want you to go and sit on that couch, then call him.'

Chance watched the woman navigate around the furniture, hugging her dressing gown tightly around her breasts. A fine-boned face with almost alabaster skin, framed by a head of long, tousled blonde hair, intelligent brown eyes that tried unsuccessfully to mask her fear.

When she was seated, she took a deep breath, called Hamilton.

'Hang on a sec, darling,' came a breezy reply from the bedroom.

Not wanting to frighten her further, Chance avoided her eyes, gazed instead at the fish tank directly behind her.

Hamilton emerged a few moments later in a terry towelling dressing gown, an empty champagne bottle in his hand. He hesitated when he recognised the fear on the woman's face, followed her eyes to Chance, froze, his mouth slightly open.

'Sit down next to her, Warwick.' Chance pointed the gun stomach level at the real estate developer.

Hamilton was almost exactly as Chance would've imagined him: dark hair, a well-proportioned, deeply tanned face.

It took the real estate developer only a moment to recompose himself. He said something to the woman as he sat that was swallowed by the classical musical, patting her knee reassuringly.

'I don't know who you are or why you are here, but I'm sure we can work—'

Before he could finish his sentence, Chance raised the gun slightly, fired. The fish tank exploded. The noise of the shot and the exploding glass was immense. Water poured out of the shattered pane of glass, drained away, leaving tiny fish flapping on the sodden carpet.

The woman screamed, clutched Hamilton's shoulder. The real estate developer jumped, put his hands up in front of him. 'Okay, okay, take whatever you want, just don't hurt us,' he pleaded.

'Your friend is safe. It's you I'm going to hurt,' said Chance. 'If you don't tell me what I want to know.'

The sound of the gunshot would have been partly muffled by the classical music, but anyone looking up from the beach below would've seen the muzzle flash. Chance had to work fast.

He walked over to the stereo and killed the sound, the gun still pointed at Hamilton.

'Where's Leigh?'

His face screwed up. 'I don't know what you mean.'

'Vera Leigh, the woman whose business you have been trying to close down for the past year. She's missing and you and your company are my number one suspects.'

Chance sensed Hamilton shifting gears, trying to put everything that was happening together, the flash of realisation as he did.

'If Leigh is missing, it has nothing to do with me.'

'You're the one who has the most to benefit from her disappearance.'

Hamilton shook his head. 'That woman has been a thorn in the side of our plans, costing my associates and me money. We may have leaned on her a little, made her life difficult in various ways, but we're not stupid enough to kidnap her.'

Chance took a step forward, the Luger still pointed at

Hamilton. 'Convince me.'

The woman cowered, flung an arm around her lover's neck. Hamilton threw her off, stared defiantly at the barrel of the Luger. 'Because it's not necessary to get what we want. It's just a matter of time before she sells to us.'

'What do you mean?'

'How much do you know about Leigh?'

Chance said nothing.

'Her business was going under long before we appeared on the scene. We're just putting her out of her misery, administering the *coup de grâce*, as it were.'

Hamilton shrugged. The confidence had returned to his face.

'White Cube Property Investment is not some bunch of street thugs. We're part of a global conglomeration with very deep pockets. We don't make a move without researching it first and anticipating every single problem and possibility. As a consequence, we know everything about Leigh and the people who work for her, including you, Mister Chance.'

Chance gripped the gun hard in an effort to hide the surprise on his face. He cussed Loomis to himself, his own stupidity in agreeing to come here.

Hamilton sat back, smiled as his words hit home.

'We even know about her efforts to chase the diamonds that are supposedly connected to a certain infamous robbery that took place in Melbourne in the seventies. It's a ridiculous story, but desperate people like her will do anything to get out of the situation they are in.'

The nagging feeling of uncertainty that had been bothering Chance suddenly felt like a rock in the pit of his stomach.

'How much do you actually know about your employer, Mister Chance?'

Chance said nothing.

'Did you know she had an affair back in the day with that man who supposedly took the diamonds, George Mundy?'

The skin on Chance's face was hot under the balaclava.

'You fucking amateur. No. I can see you didn't. Rumour has it, she even had a child by him, who was given up for adoption.'

Chance sprang towards Hamilton, swiped the butt of the Lugar across the man's nose. He cried out in pain.

The woman screamed, lunged at Chance. He grabbed her by the wrist with his free hand, pushed her away. She fell to the floor, lay there weeping.

Blood gushed from Hamilton's nostrils, spread web-like on his face. Chance pushed the Luger's barrel into Hamilton's mouth, heard the metal clink against his teeth.

'I made a mistake coming here,' Chance said. 'This can end tonight, and you can go on with your affairs, including your plans for Leigh's business, as if nothing happened and you'll never see me again. You go to the police or I notice anyone I don't know suddenly paying attention to me, I promise, I'll blow a hole in your life you could drive a semi-trailer through. Do you understand me?'

Beads of sweat had appeared on Hamilton's face, mixed with the blood. He squirmed against the gun barrel.

'Nod that you fucking understand,' Chance said, his hands trembling.

Hamilton nodded as best he could with the gun in his mouth.

Chance withdrew the gun barrel, brought it down hard against the side of Hamilton's head. The developer slumped unconscious on the couch.

The woman screamed, crawled across the carpet towards her lover. Chance ignored her, scanned the floor for the spent cartridge from the round he'd put into the fish tank. He found it, snatched it up, made like hell out of the house, down the stairs, and towards the outline of the boat waiting for him in the water.

SIX

Everything about Mudcrab gave Hardigan the shits. His stupid nickname, the spidery tattoos that covered his scrawny arms, the acrid smell of his body odour, most of all, his constant chatter.

The scrawny little fucker lounged in Hardigan's favourite recliner, wearing track suit pants and a blue wifebeater singlet, necking a can of beer, oblivious to the old man's baleful glare, as he explained to Celeste the importance of white civilisation making sure it wasn't outbred by mongrel races.

Christ on a crutch, but there's one mongrel I can see in this room, thought Hardigan darkly, as he paced the room. His police service issue Colt .32 sat in a shoulder holster under his left arm. Both the weapon and the holster dated back to Hardigan's time with Victoria's Armed Robbery Squad and had been lovingly cared for in the years since. Hardigan pondered the pros and cons of taking his pistol out, putting a bullet right between Mudcrab's beady eyes, shutting him the fuck up for good.

Hardigan breathed deeply, turned his attention instead to the others arranged around the loungeroom of his farmhouse.

Tremont, cunning but clearly terrified of the company he now found himself in, was the easiest to control. While Hardigan doubted Tremont might find a clown in a circus, he couldn't fault his memory. Tremont had supplied Hardigan with a surprisingly accurate layout of Leigh's sprawling apartment complex, based on recollections from a couple of her parties he'd attended.

Hardigan could tell by the tatts that peeked out from Swain's T-shirt the big man shared Mudcrab's worldview but was smart enough to keep his politics to himself, at least around Hardigan. That was all Hardigan needed for now. He had Swain pegged as tough and reliable as far as it went, and as far as it went was the prospect of getting his share of the diamonds.

Celeste came across as impressionable and unpredictable. Hardigan noticed by the way Tremont looked at her they'd had a thing once, but whatever it was, she was Swain's woman now. Hardigan had known more than a few females like Celeste in his time, women who compensated for low self-esteem by being in the thrall of more powerful, often violent men.

Hardigan had bought the farmhouse, located in thick bushland in central Victoria, after he'd left the police force back in the early nineties. He and Kieu had lived happily there in what had turned out to be the last decade of her life. It almost felt like a betrayal of those memories to bring these people here, but there was no choice.

He couldn't very well stash Leigh in that dump Mudcrab called home. He needed somewhere secluded while he sweated her for information and formulated his next steps. Besides, he felt Kieu would've understood the need to make sacrifices. She'd made enough in her own life.

The idea to take the Mundy woman and Leigh had come to him while he'd knelt in front of the shrine to Kieu that sat against one of the walls in his bedroom. The room was strictly off limits to his guests.

Hardigan didn't really understand the concept of ancestor worship or believe in talking to ghosts and that they could talk back. But Kieu had made him promise to keep a shrine to her, telling him repeatedly while foreigners believed only in death, the Vietnamese believed in the dead, and she would always be with him.

He wasn't sure what she had meant, but he'd kept his word, regularly left fruit and sweets in front of the framed black and white photograph of his late wife. It was taken the first day she'd arrived in Australia, her eyes brimming with a mix of excitement to be reunited with him and anxiety at suddenly being in a strange country. Sometimes, he even lit one of the joss sticks he kept in a small clay pot. He liked the smell, found it calming.

So far, as much seemed to be going wrong with his plan as right.

How was he to know Sylvia Mundy had had a bad heart, or whatever it was that meant that the dose of chloroform they'd given her as they bundled her out of her home had killed her. She'd taken whatever information she had to her shallow grave amid a clump of eucalyptus on the eastern side of his property.

Tied up in Hardigan's spare room, Vera Leigh was made of tougher stuff. Snatching her had gone largely to plan. Tremont and Celeste had stayed in his Kombi van, the engine running. Mudcrab had been sent in first to cut the power. Hardigan and Swain had made their way to Leigh's quarters and grabbed her. The gaunt old tart had put up quite a fight but nothing that couldn't be dealt with by a quick rabbit punch in the face.

Hardigan was not worried about the bodyguard's death. After all it was not as though Leigh's friends could go to the police. Truth be told, he was surprised Mudcrab had the bottle to kill someone.

But the woman he bragged about throwing down the disused elevator shaft, getting a superficial knife wound for his trouble—that was another matter.

Hardigan had followed the woman one time, on a trip to the State Library, where she had spent an afternoon reading. She was older than Tremont had described her, attractive, with a hair style that reminded Hardigan of the Sharpie girls he used to bust in the early nineteen seventies when he was still in uniform.

She was with Chance, according to Tremont, and Hardigan *was* worried about him. Tremont had filled him in on the little he knew about Gary Chance, including the botched plastic surgery job.

Hardigan had got a mate's son who was in the force to pull up anything else on him. Time in the army, including tours in East Timor and Afghanistan, but zero criminal record. That told Hardigan Chance was smart, careful and a potential threat to his plans.

Hardigan had been looking for the diamonds on and off for going on three decades. Chasing down old crims, mostly all dead now, tracking down rumours and whispers that had turned out to be nothing.

He'd even gone as far as flying to Manila to check out the bar owned by that fat prick, Grove. Hardigan got major Saigon era flashbacks from the foreign men sitting around a raised stage, ogling a bunch of Filipinas in skimpy bikinis who looked like it hadn't been more than a week or two since they left the farm in whatever backwoods part of the archipelago they hailed from.

But now he was onto something concrete for the first time since the actual Great Bookie Robbery. Leigh had already told him what she knew about the Great Bookie Robbery, her relationship with Mundy, even the child they'd had together, which she'd admitted putting up for adoption. Leigh had been particularly reticent to talk about the last point, however, which made Hardigan think she was sitting on more information.

Those diamonds, if they existed—they had to exist—were Hardigan's retirement package, and he was buggered if he was going to let Leigh, Chance or anyone else stand in the way of him cashing in.

His thoughts were interrupted by a renewed tirade on the part of Mudcrab. Some bullshit about the Aboriginal welfare complex.

The only Aborigine Hardigan had ever been close to was a young bloke called Vince—he couldn't remember his second name—who hailed from somewhere in Queensland. Vince was another tunnel rat in Vietnam and one of the bravest sappers Hardigan had known. Vince was often the first to go down a tunnel shaft. He was completely unafraid of the claustrophobia, the lack of oxygen, the possible booby traps, and the tear gas the Australians pumped into the tunnels to clear them of VC, the remnants burning the exposed skin on your hands and neck.

Hardigan ran a trembling hand through his thinning sandy coloured hair, recalled the racist jokes the other sappers made at Vince's expense, the favourite being how he was so black the VC wouldn't see him coming along the tunnel.

Hardigan wasn't political, never had been, but over half a century later he still felt a ripple of shame for not speaking up in Vince's defence. There was an Aboriginal man, risking his life for a country that at the time didn't even recognise him as a citizen, being made fun of by white men who exchanged scraps of food for sex with the hungry Vietnamese women who would wait near the wire around the base at Nui Dat.

Hardigan wondered where Vince was now. He felt his body grow hot, the trembling in his hands become worse. Mudcrab's voice became a distant murmur in his head. In a fumbling movement, Hardigan drew the Colt, fired. The shot was impossibly loud in the confined space of the lounge room. The back of Mudcrab's head exploded and he slumped in the recliner, finally silent.

A fine red mist clung to the air momentarily as the others stared at Hardigan wide eyed, not daring to move. Hardigan met each of their stares in turn, paused on Swain, arched an eyebrow in a silent challenge. Swain nodded warily to him.

'Clean up the mess and bury this piece of shit next to the Mundy woman,' Hardigan said, holstering his pistol. 'I'm going to sweat Leigh some more.'

SEVEN

When Chance woke, the worst of his shakes were over. He lay twisted in the sheets, his pillow damp with sweat.

The Bangkok doctor who treated the malaria Chance had picked up on the Thai-Burma border hadn't finished the job. The parasite remained in his body, and every now and again sent him a reminder of its presence.

It took a moment to recognise his room in Leigh's apartment complex. Daylight peeked through a crack in the thick drapes. Slowly, he recalled the events of the previous night. Was it the previous night? How long had he been out of it?

He remembered wading through the cold swell in front of Hamilton's house, climbing into the boat, only having the energy for a brief expletive laden report back to Loomis before sprawling exhausted against the side of the boat.

Loomis had kept his own counsel as he piloted the craft, the wind sending his hair streaming behind him. Chance had angled his head over the side of the boat, let the sea spray cool his burning skin.

He reached for his tobacco, laid out with the other contents of his pockets on the bedside table. He couldn't remember putting them there. He rolled a cigarette, sat naked on the edge of the bed, mulled over the job in his mind as he smoked.

That he was satisfied the real estate developer had been telling the truth was no comfort.

Not only did they still not have any no idea where Leigh was, she'd lied to them about her relationship with Mundy. The real estate developer's last words rang through the fog in his mind. She and Mundy had had a relationship, maybe even a child. What on earth was she doing, asking him to track Mundy down? What else hadn't she told them?

More disturbing from Chance's point of view was he'd been identified. He wasn't naive. Modern surveillance technology made it inevitable that his face flashed across countless screens of numerous state authorities every day. The trick was to avoid the red flags that drew official attention. Attention which once it started would peel away his false identity as John Egan, or any other he might choose, as easily as removing the skin from an onion.

That meant being prepared and careful. Working in small groups, whenever possible, with people he knew and trusted. It meant not doing a job unless he was sure of the reliability of his associates. In short, it meant not being caught. Chance had no official record aside from that arising from his time in the army, and he meant to keep it that way.

Taking the occasional risk or shortcut was unavoidable. But the current job, especially going to America, had entailed far more danger than he was comfortable with. Last night—whatever night it had been—when they braced Hamilton was a wake-up call. He felt bad for Leigh, but the fact she'd lied to him neutralised any guilty feeling.

A strange calm came over him as the decision took shape in his mind. He was out.

He was pondering the best way to untangle himself from the job when Loomis appeared in the doorway.

'Well, here you are, hale and hearty,' Loomis said with a wolfish grin. He wore a pinstriped suit coat and pants, scuffed shoes with Cuban heels, a white shirt, and his trade-mark cravat, deep burgundy, neatly tucked in the collar.

'How long have I been out of it?'

'The better part of two days. You really should get that malaria treated properly.'

Chance nodded.

Loomis opened the curtains. Sunlight poured in, cut through the funk of sickness. 'It's a glorious day. Shall we meet on the patio?'

Chance sniffed, ran a hand over his face. He smelled rank and needed a shave.

'Let me clean up first.'

Chance sat in a cane chair. Despite being hemmed in by buildings on every side, late autumn sunlight bathed the patio in a drowsy warmth. The sound of the traffic was a distant thrum, like large insects in the air.

The patio was occupied by a collection of furniture, much of it in serious disrepair, and ringed with garden beds and pots, the plants wilted and dead.

Chance waved away Loomis's offer of food but accepted a drink, a concoction of water mixed with sugar, salt, ginger and lemon.

'You don't have as many hangovers as I've had lad, without coming up with a decent way of rehydrating.' Loomis perched expectantly on the edge of a garden beds next to statue of what looked like two cherubs fucking.

Chance was surprised by the unusually solicitous tone in the old man's words, wondered if he felt guilty about the abortive visit to the real estate developer or whether another agenda was behind his kindness.

Chance drained the last of the drink and lit a cigarette as Eva emerged through the French doors, a laptop and a manila folder under her arm.

'Hey, you,' she said, bending over to kiss him, her tongue lingering on his.

'Hey yourself.'

'How are you feeling?'

'Better, thanks.'

She looked good in faded black jeans and a white T-shirt. He felt a stirring in his groin, wondered what future they had if they were no longer working the same job.

Eva sat in a matching cane chair opposite Chance.

'I've been looking into Hamilton's claim Vera had a child with Mundy.'

Chance nodded, feigning interest.

'The Bookie Robbery took place in April 1976, and we know Mundy left the country later that year. The most logical assumption is Leigh, either not wanting to have to look after a child or thinking she couldn't, gave it up for adoption as a baby, sometime in the late seventies.

'If this was the case, and assuming she put the child up for adoption in Victoria,' she paused, pursed her lips as she consulted the notes in her folder, 'there were over one hundred and fifty children's and babies' homes, hostels and orphanages operating in the state at that time. We might do a freedom of information request to the Department of Health and Human Services to find out which one it was. But even if we somehow got around the privacy issues, it could take months to get an answer. Even then, we may come up with nothing.'

'In other words,' Chance said, drawing on the last of his cigarette and dropping the stub into the empty glass at his feet, 'it's like searching for a needle in a haystack.'

'I'm afraid so,' said Eva.

'Besides, I don't see any connection between the diamonds and the fact Leigh got rid of her child with Mundy because she couldn't be arsed looking after it.' Chance felt anger welling up inside him. 'That's aside from the question of why she omitted to tell us she'd had a child with the man we've spent the last few weeks trying to track down. She's not only lied to us, she's put us all in danger.'

'Her lifestyle back in those days was hardly conducive with

childrearing,' Loomis said gently. 'That hardly makes her unique. There would've been a lot of women faced with the same heartbreaking decision in those days.'

Chance suddenly sat up straight. 'Where I left my heart,' he said, almost as if to himself.

'I don't understand what you mean, Gary,' Eva said.

'Maybe our friend is still delirious from the effects of the malaria,' Loomis said.

Chance stood up and went inside. Taking the stairs two at a time, he entered Leigh's quarters, scanning the room until he saw what he wanted.

He re-emerged onto the patio holding a framed picture, a little smaller than a piece of A4 paper.

'What is it?' Eva said.

Chance held the picture in front of his companions. The frame contained a simple pencil drawing of an old building.

Loomis and Eva looked at each other and then expectantly back to him.

'It's a drawing by Leigh,' said Chance flipping the frame over. 'I suddenly remembered asking her where it was, and she answered the place I left my heart or something similar. She was drunk and I figured she was rambling.'

The back of the frame was held in place by brown paper, brittle with age and starting to come away on one side. Chance easily inserted a finger in the existing tear and gently ripped it away to reveal a hollow space containing what looked like an old administration document of some kind.

Chance squinted at the form, found the faded spidery handwriting almost illegible. 'I can't make this out.' He handed it to Eva.

Eva silently mouthed the words as she read.

'It says a Miss Vera Leigh gave up a three-year-old boy, James Leigh, into the care of a Catholic run orphanage called Broadmoor Lodge for Boys, in September 1979.'

'Well, that's one mystery solved,' Chance said, folding his

arms. 'But it doesn't make any difference to me. I've been doing some thinking and I've had enough of this job. I'm out.'

'"Though those that are betray'd do feel the treason sharply, ye traitor stands in worse case of woe",' said Loomis softly. 'This is the first I've heard about the child, also. But as aggrieved as I am by her duplicity, Gary, I still will not judge her.'

'You can quote Shakespeare, or whoever the hell that is, as much as you like. I don't owe Leigh anything. I should've recognised from her behaviour she was desperate to save her business at any cost. That was my mistake. But Angel's dead and I was nearly killed in America because of Leigh.'

Chance held up his still bandaged hand to emphasise the point.

'And now I discover this Hamilton guy, a total stranger, appears to know more about the job we are working than we do. Far worse than that, he's made me and knows I work for Leigh.'

'You're not the only person whose life has been threatened,' said Eva. 'Have you forgotten, I nearly got thrown down an elevator shaft. And do I also have to remind you I wouldn't even be here now if it wasn't for what happened up north, the score I was working on you stumbled into the middle of and nearly got both of us killed...'

'Oh Christ, we're not going to go through this again—'

'Besides, did you think recovering ninety million in diamonds from a heist that happened almost half a century ago would be easy?'

'Even if the story is true, this stuff about Leigh putting up her child for adoption, I don't see how it gets us any closer to the diamonds.'

'This exchange you had with Vera, about her drawing,' said Loomis. 'Can you remember exactly what she said?'

'I don't know, it was a while ago and, like I said, she was drunk and not making any sense.'

'Think, Gary.'

'When I asked her about the picture, all she said was it was where she'd left her heart. Then she added, "amongst other things".

'Oh, no, absolutely not.' Chance saw by the sparkle in Eva's eyes exactly what she was thinking. 'By other things I'm sure she didn't mean the diamonds.'

'How do you know?' said Eva intently. 'At least admit it's another part of the puzzle, another link to Mundy. Aren't you the least bit curious about all of this, why Leigh lied to us, what she is hiding?'

'Admittedly, her mental health is clearly declining. But why would she be prepared to pay us such a large amount of money to find diamonds, the location of which is in a clue right under her very nose. It makes no sense.

'And as for being a link to Mundy, he's dead and buried under a hardware barn somewhere in suburban Pennsylvania.' Chance was unsure whether he was trying to convince the others or himself.

'But you never saw his body, you said so yourself. You don't know for certain he's dead.'

'Do you realise how desperate you sound?'

'Better than most. I grew up around desperate people, my mother, who took off as soon as she could, my bullshit bank robber of a father and his dodgy mates. Yeah, I'm desperate. I can't afford not to be. I'm a nearly forty-year-old woman with bugger-all prospects. My share would set me up for life. I intend to find the diamonds with or without you.'

Chance made a balloon of his cheek, exhaled loudly. 'What about you, old man? Do you go along with this craziness?'

Loomis nodded.

'What about this Broadmoor Lodge for Boys? Does it still exist?'

Eva opened her laptop, tapped at the keyboard. Chance rolled himself another cigarette, had nearly finished it when Eva looked up at him.

'It was closed after a fire in the late eighties. There were also allegations of abuse against the priest in charge, a Father Gleeson. But the building still exists, about one hundred and fifty kilometres west of Ballarat, on the edge of the Grampians National Park.'

Eva turned the screen towards Chance. Loomis stood up from his perch and peered over Chance's shoulder. The building on the screen was unmistakably the same as the one in Leigh's sketch. A double-storey structure with a slate roof, two large brick buildings on either side, connected by a middle section with rooms running off it, an enclosed wooden veranda on both levels. The building on the right had an arched entranceway. Thick bush encroached on either side. In the foreground, several tiny figures were dwarfed by the entrance.

For some reason, the image made Chance think about his own family, his parents, long dead, a brother with whom he had nothing in common, whom he hadn't seen since before he joined the army, who wouldn't even recognise him now.

'Even if this is the same place as the building in Leigh's drawing, I don't see how this information gets you any closer to the diamonds,' said Chance, rolling another cigarette. 'It's certainly not going to help you find Vera or Sylvia Mundy.'

'There's the priest, Gleeson. What if he's still alive and still in Ballarat? If so, he might know something about the boy.' Eva sighed. 'I know it's not much, but it's all we have. This and the neighbour's descriptions of the people who were seen taking Sylvia Mundy from her home.'

'That's the first I've heard of any descriptions,' said Chance. 'Tell me exactly, what did the neighbour say?'

'The neighbour, a young woman with a baby, was vague. It was night, and she saw Sylvia leaving with two men. She didn't get a look at one, the other was broad and bald, with what looked like tattoos on his arms.'

Chance felt like he'd been slapped in the face.

'Swain,' he said under his breath.

'What?'

'Broad, bald, and an armful of tattoos, who does that remind you of?'

'Swain, you're right,' said Eva. 'That Nazi fuck.'

'A Nazi?' said Loomis. 'I hate Nazis.'

'It's been staring us in the face the entire time,' said Chance. 'Swain took Sylvia, probably Vera as well. I don't know why, revenge for what happened up north or another angle he's playing. Maybe he's heard about the diamonds, too, wants to squeeze both women for information.'

'But how did he know to follow us here?' said Eva.

'Loomis, how much did Tremont know about Leigh? Has he ever been here, maybe attended one of her parties?'

'Yes, I believe he might've come to one or two of Vera's soirees. But I always acted as the cut-out in whatever dealings we've had with Tremont, so he's never actually met her. Besides, he's a second-rate player at best. I wouldn't have thought he was up to heavy stuff like kidnapping.'

'No, but Swain is. Tremont just provided the background information that led him to Melbourne after us and into this building to get Leigh.'

Chance lit another cigarette, his mind going over the implications.

'The exact details don't matter. We need to close the loop on Swain and whoever he's working with. Whether or not the diamonds are real, finding them or some trace of them lets us locate Swain. And when we do, we can get him out of our lives for good.'

'Yes, my friends, let's scrub his soul from the list of the living.'

Chance exhaled in a sigh. 'Looks like I'm back in after all.'

EIGHT

Once they'd cleared Melbourne traffic, the Falcon had made good time to Ballarat. Loomis resembled a grizzled World War I fighter ace as he sat behind the steering wheel in an old leather jacket and silk scarf. Eva, in the front passenger seat next to him, recited her latest research from notes on her lap.

Chance listened from the back seat, watched the paddocks and hills roll past. As uncertain as he was the trip would lead to anything, it felt good to at least be out and on the move after being bedridden for several days.

'Around two dozen boys between the ages of three and sixteen lived at Broadmoor at any one time,' said Eva. 'This Father Gleeson, the priest in charge, was there the night a mysterious fire ripped through the place sometime in 1989. No one knows how it started, but a couple of staff died. Gleeson was left with serious injuries.

'The official story was Gleeson retired soon after due to wounds sustained in the fire, but rumours he was involved in abuse started circulating soon after.' Eva opened her mouth to read from her notes, changed her mind. 'I don't need to go into all the details. No charges were ever laid against him, and the brazen fucker still lives in Ballarat.'

'How do you know all this?' said Chance.

'I have my sources.' Eva grinned over her shoulder at him. 'Actually, there was a fair bit in the media about the accusations against Gleeson. One of the advocacy groups working with victims of child sexual assault in the Catholic church slipped me his address on the sly, said to do whatever we wanted as long as nothing could be traced back to them.'

Loomis parked the Falcon in front of a run-down cream brick block of flats on the outskirts of Ballarat. Overstuffed green wheelie bins formed a crooked line along a cracked concrete path leading to the entrance. The overgrown lawn was dotted with yellow flowers, a dash of colour which made the location appear marginally less dismal.

Loomis stayed with the car as Eva and Chance wound their way between bags of rubbish that hadn't quite made it as far as the bins to Gleeson's ground-floor flat.

Eva was about to knock for a third time when the door slowly opened, and an old man, his face covered in snow white whiskers, peered out from the gloom.

'Yes?' His voice was a dry whisper.

As previously arranged, Eva took the lead.

'Mister Thomas Gleeson?'

The old man nodded.

'Good morning, Mister Gleeson, my associate and I were wondering whether we might have a word with you about your time at the Broadmoor Lodge for Boys?'

'I have nothing to say,' said the old man, trying to shut the door as he slipped back into the darkness.

Eva wedged a booted foot in the crack of the door to prevent the old man closing it, easily pushed it open with the weight of her body and stepped inside. Chance glanced around to make sure they had not attracted attention from any of the neighbours, and when he was satisfied no one was watching, joined Eva inside.

Gleeson stood crookedly in the middle of a dimly lit room. His clothes hung loosely from his gaunt frame. He was completely bald. Deep wrinkles lined the papery skin on his face, fleshy sacks under his watery eyes. He smelled unwashed.

It took Chance a moment to register the old man was leaning

on a walking stick, one damaged leg protruding at an odd angle from the rest of his body.

Chance had expected the flat to be a mess, but the dim light from a single lampshade illuminated a spotless living space, a couple of pieces of furniture, worn shag pile carpet, a blanket over the window. A kitchen was visible off one side of the room, a closed door, presumably to a bedroom, off another. The only decoration was a crucifix on the wall.

It was the place of someone waiting to die.

'I don't want to talk to you,' said the old man curtly. 'Please leave or I'll have no choice but to call the police.'

'No, I don't think you will do that, Mister Gleeson,' said Eva, taking a step towards him. 'Not unless you want your neighbours to find out they live in the same block of flats as a paedophile.'

'Nothing was ever proven.'

'Cut the bullshit. We know exactly who you are and what you did. I don't know why the hell you're not in jail. Some cosy deal between you and the other kiddie fiddlers in the church, no doubt. Lucky for you, that's not why we're here. We just want information about one of the boys at Broadmoor. You give us that, and we'll leave you to what little is left of your miserable life.'

The old man's lips moved like a fish out of water, but no sound came out.

'Now sit the fuck down on that couch and get ready to answer some questions. And if I think you are lying, I'll hurt you while my friend here takes a spray can to the outside of this miserable block of flats, decorates it with an update about where people can find their local, neighbourhood pedo. Understand?'

The old man moved crablike on his walking stick, sat awkwardly on the couch, his hands at his sides, his bad leg sticking out in front of him.

Chance grabbed two chairs from the Formica table in the kitchen, brought them into the living room for him and Eva.

'A woman dropped off a boy called James Leigh in 1979,' Eva said firmly. 'He would have been three. What can you tell us about him and what happened to him?'

At the mention of the boy's name, the old man's lower lip quivered. A rivulet of sweat ran down the crags of his cheek.

'Nothing...I don't know anything.'

'You're going to have to do better than that.' Eva reached down and slid out a double-bladed knife from a sheaf in her boot, held it directly in front of Gleeson's face.

Chance tensed, unsure where things were going. The ex-priest's eyes became wide, and there was a discernible tremor in one of his hands.

'I'll ask one more time. James Leigh. What do you know about him and where he went?'

'I never heard the name,' Gleeson said, gulping air between each word, beads of sweat popping across his bald pate. 'Please, in the name of God, I swear I know nothing.'

In one quick fluid movement, Eva flipped the hilt of the knife over, so she was holding the blade down, plunged it into the centre of the wooden coffee table separating her and Gleeson.

'God stopped listening to anything you had to say to him a long time ago,' said Eva icily. 'Now, listen to me, you piece of shit, because this is the last time I ask nicely. The boy. What do you know about him? Spill or so help me, I'll start carving pieces off you, starting with the shrivelled little pecker you used to force the orphans to touch.'

Chance stopped himself from stepping in and restraining Eva, trusting she knew what she was doing.

'I wasn't there the night his mother dropped him off, and I don't remember much about him,' said Gleeson. 'He was just another snotty brat dropped off by some slut who couldn't look after the precious life she'd brought into the world. It was our job to teach the children Christian devotion. Sometimes those methods were harsh, true. We had to beat the devil out of them.'

'Was it necessary to fuck them as well?'

The old man squirmed, not meeting Eva's stare, clasped and unclasped his hands on his lap.

'No, we only gave them discipline.'

Chance watched Eva breathe deeply in an effort to control herself.

'But I was there the night the dark man came to take the boy away.'

Eva flicked Chance a quick look, her eyebrows raised. Chance gave her an almost perceptible nod in return.

'Took Jamie away?'

Gleeson nodded hard several times.

'Who was the dark man?'

'I don't know his name. It was night. He was wreathed in shadow. He brought fire with him and did this to me.' The old man indicated at his crooked leg. 'Shot me in the kneecap.' The old man started to unbutton his shirt as he spoke. 'And then when he found out what I did to the boys, to Jamie, he gave me this.'

Gleeson arced his head back, opened his shirt wide, and thrust his pale, sunken chest toward her. The gesture, almost sexual, exposed the jagged welts of letters carved into his chest.

Eva recoiled. 'What the fuck does that say?'

'Rockspider,' said Chance. 'Underworld slang for paedophile.'

'The dark man said, while he wanted to kill me, it was better I live with all the world knowing what I am.' Gleeson gently closed his shirt, wrapped his arms tightly around himself, smiled coquettishly at the two of them.

'Then he left with Jamie, and I never saw either of them again.'

The old man didn't move, staring into the space in between his two captors for a moment. Then a fearful demeanour returned to his old features, and he shrank back against the couch.

'Please don't hurt me,' he said. 'The other men who came here asking about Jamie, they said they wouldn't hurt me if I told them what I knew. And now that I've told you, you won't hurt me either, will you?'

'What other men?' Chance stood as he spoke.

Gleeson cowered, pushing himself against the back of the couch.

'What other men?' Chance repeated louder.

'There were two of them. One was tall and old, had a bearing like a soldier. The other was bald and covered with strange tattoos. They didn't give me their names, but they wanted to know about the Leigh boy, too.'

'When was this?'

'Yesterday.'

'And you didn't think to tell us this?' Chance realised how stupid the question was as soon as he said it.

The old man wiped the sweat from his upper lip, looked up at Chance uncomprehendingly.

'We're not going to get anything more out of him,' said Chance. 'Let's get out of here.'

Eva stood, put her foot on the coffee table as she prised the knife from the wood and slid it back into her boot. She gave the still cowering ex-priest a contemptuous look and followed.

'Whoever did that to him was right,' Eva said as she caught up with Chance as he strode across the overgrown lawn. 'That sack of shit deserves to suffer.'

Chance grunted. He'd already left Gleeson behind, focused on their next move.

'If this dark man Gleeson was jabbering about is Mundy, that's one riddle solved,' Chance said. 'Whoever it is lying under the mall in Pennsylvania, it's not our man. Mundy's still alive or at least was back in 1989. Somehow, he found out what was going on at Broadmoor and came to rescue his son.'

He stopped and turned to Eva.

'Swain and whoever else he is working with are following exactly the same leads as we are in the hope it'll bring them closer to Mundy and the diamonds. If you were Swain and received the information we just did, what would your next move be?'

She ran the fingers of one of her hands backward and forward across the tips of the overgrown lawn as she thought.

'If they've come this far, Broadmoor orphanage. Definitely. Maybe to look for any leads that might shed light on where Mundy went. At the very least, just to check the place out.'

'Well, we have nothing to lose by having a look,' Chance consulted his watch. 'It's midday. If we leave now, we can make it by three. That'll give a few hours of daylight to case the place.'

NINE

The drive to the Broadmoor Lodge for Boys wound through partly forested country. The trees had lost their leaves as winter approached, exposing their gnarled branches to sky, which turned slate grey as the day drew to a close.

Loomis stopped the car at the turnoff to a potholed single lane road bordered by thick bush, the asphalt crumbling away at the edges. Mobile phone reception, patchy for the last hour of their journey, ceased completely, but an old metal sign with the words 'Orphan Road', told them they were close to Broadmoor.

The three of them sat there for a moment, listened to the car's V8 engine purr, then Loomis turned the car and piloted it down the road, steering to avoid the largest of the potholes.

Chance thought about the young boys who had made the same journey in the past. Some, those old enough to realise what was happening, would have been gripped in fear. Others, the sons of violent men or parents too poor or dysfunctional to raise them, maybe had higher hopes, only to discover they were trading one version of hell for another.

The bush became thicker, almost felt like it was closing in on them, until the road ended at a rusty chain-link fence. A faded metal sign, peppered with shotgun spray, announced, 'Private Property: Trespassers Will Be Prosecuted'.

Loomis pulled into a clearing at the side of the road and killed the engine as Chance got out and inspected the gate. He

173

fingered what looked like a suspiciously new link of chain and padlock that secured the gate.

'I don't suppose we have a pair of bolt cutters with us?' he said to no one in particular.

Loomis shook his head.

Chance peered through the chain link. The asphalt stopped at the gate. On the other side, a dirt road veered left and disappeared behind thick bush. Chance thought he could make out what looked like fresh tyre tracks in the moist soil.

Chance went to the car's glove box, checked the Luger was loaded, and slipped it in between his jeans and the small of his back.

'We have at least a couple more hours of sunlight,' he said between gulps from a plastic bottle of water. 'Let's reconnoitre the fence, see if there's another way to get in.'

Chance passed the water to Eva, who finished it off. They waited on the edge of the clearing while Loomis popped the boot. 'Give me a moment to tool up, will you?' he said.

Loomis placed an army surplus haversack on the car roof. He closed the boot, slung the haversack over one shoulder, some sort of gun cradled in his arms.

'Is that what I think it is, old man?' said Chance.

'If that would be a Sten gun, then yes, correct my boy.' Loomis fitted a magazine into the side of the barrel, banged the end of it with his palm to lock it into place.

'What are you going to do with it? Shoot Germans?'

Loomis arched a crooked eyebrow, grinned. 'Didn't you two say this chap Swain is some kind of Nazi, so, yes, close enough.'

'No bolt cutters, but there's a spare can of petrol and some food in the boot.' Loomis knelt on the ground as he spoke, pulled out what looked like a pair of binoculars from the knapsack. 'Also thought these might also come in handy. Night vision goggles. Not military grade, but good enough for our purposes.'

'You're not as useless as you look, Loomis,' said Eva, smiling.

'Thank you, Miss McCullough.' Loomis gave her a slight

bow. 'Let's go for a ramble, shall we?'

They followed the chain-link fence through the thick bush, walking in single file until they came to a hole big enough for an adult to climb through. It had been made some time ago, the tips where the wire was cut rusted smooth by the elements. Empty spray cans and beer bottles lay in the grass nearby.

The landscape on the other side was dotted with gum and tea trees. Pink-white corellas and sulphur-crested cockatoos screeched from the foliage.

The bush thinned out until the rear of the orphanage building became visible about fifty metres away. Much of the brickwork was daubed in graffiti. Tiles were missing in patches from the roof. One wing of the building was completely derelict, the damage from the fire clearly visible.

To one side of the building was an overgrown cemetery. A collection of crooked head stones bobbed up from the bush, railed off by a wrought-iron fence. No doubt the final resting place for those young wards not strong enough to survive the horrors their adult keepers inflicted them to.

'What a place to put a child,' said Chance under his breath.

Keeping to the tree line, they circled back in the direction they'd come, until the front of the building came into view. The wooden doors of the arched entranceway stood open, a large four-wheel drive and a Volkswagen Kombi Van parked out the front.

'Swain and his conspirators have indeed got here before us,' said Loomis.

To their left was a slight rise where a large fallen gum lay, the rotting wood streaked with dry moss. Chance decided it would make a suitable vantage point for watching the orphanage and motioned the others to follow him.

The three of them crouched behind the tree, waiting in anticipation for a sign of who was inside. They tensed as they heard voices. A tall man emerged, barked an order to someone who hadn't yet appeared, then opened the sliding door on the van.

The tall man was fair-haired and old, but there was something about his demeanour, even from a distance: what Chance had once heard an American marine in Afghanistan refer to as command presence.

A slightly dishevelled figure stumbled out of the front door, looked around if he was lost.

'Isn't that the guy from the roadside, that night at Cornelius's commune?' Eva said.

'My old partner, Tremont,' said Chance. 'That solves the mystery of how Swain tracked us to Melbourne.'

'And how they got into the apartment complex to take Leigh,' said Loomis, the barrel of his Sten resting on the top of the log. 'Do you think my employer is with them?'

'Maybe.'

The tall man withdrew a sledgehammer from the vehicle, passed it to Tremont.

'What do you think they're doing?' said Eva.

'It looks like they're tearing the place apart.'

'What for?'

'I don't know,' said Chance. 'Maybe they believe the diamonds are stashed in there.'

The tall man re-emerged from inside the van with a sleeping bag under each arm, carried them inside.

'If Vera is in there, we have to get her out,' Loomis said.

'Whatever, this is our opportunity to take Swain off the board for good,' Chance said as he scanned the building and its surrounds. 'We have to take it.'

The veranda and windows were boarded with sheets of corrugated iron, but he noticed what appeared to be a cellar door to the side of the entrance.

'There's two of them for certain, three if we assume Swain is somewhere inside. Maybe more. I wouldn't mind shaving the odds a little more in our favour.'

He turned around, sat against the trunk. Loomis and Eva crouched in front of him expectantly.

'They're not going anywhere for now, so we can at least wait until tonight to make any move.'

While he spoke, Chance reached for Loomis's knapsack, took out the night goggles.

'Loomis, you and Eva go back to the car, move it from the entrance to that clearing on the side of the road we saw about two kilometres back, try and camouflage it as best you can. Then grab the food, that can of petrol you mentioned, any rags you can find. If you have a crowbar, even a tyre iron, bring that, too.

'And if you've got anymore magazines for that Sten, grab them,' he said as Loomis started to move off. 'You're going to need them.'

Chance held Eva gently by the arm before she could move.

'You don't have to do this, you know?'

'Do I look like I need you to look out for me?'

'I'm just saying this is not a game. It's going to get very rough. You sure you're up for it?'

Eva nodded, leant forward and kissed him, her lips lingering on his.

'I've been thinking,' she whispered, kissing his cheek and neck, 'after this is over, what say we go somewhere, see if we can make you and I more than a sympathy fuck.'

'Or we could just walk away now.'

'I meant what I said about getting my share of the diamonds,' she said sharply, then caught herself, her green eyes softening. 'Besides, we'd get a lot further with our cut, go anywhere we wanted, do it in style.'

'Sure,' he said, letting go of her arm. 'Now go help Loomis.'

Chance knew there was no point arguing with her. He had worked with people in whom the desire for a score had overruled all sense of the risks involved. He watched her disappear into undergrowth as the gathering dusk squeezed the light from the sky.

TEN

Chance scanned the orphanage again through the night vision goggles. The sounds of people methodically taking the inside of the building apart, clearly audible across the stretch of land between the orphanage and the tree line, had ceased a couple of hours earlier.

The tall man hadn't reappeared since his last trip to get sleeping bags from the van. Tremont also hadn't resurfaced while Chance had been watching, but he had clocked Swain and a woman, Tremont's girlfriend, Celeste.

Chance switched off the goggles, conscious of not wanting to run down the battery, and pushed them up on his head. The world returned from ghostly negative to a cloudy night sky.

He crouched down to fire up a cigarette, leaned against the tree trunk, out of sight of anyone who might be watching and notice the ember. Loomis and Eva sat against the tree, both lost in their own thoughts.

Images of his time in Afghanistan had drifted into his mind as he'd watched the orphanage. Chance had met vets who had been profoundly damaged by the conflict, physically and mentally. Men who would panic at the sight of an unattended bag, who always watched the door any place they went. Chance never judged them, knew the trauma was real, but it was not him.

He'd done one rotation, mostly spent behind razor wire at the Australian army base in Tarin Kowt, Uruzgan province, in the central part of the country. Tedium, for the most part, broken only by the burst of adrenaline when he roared out of the gate at the wheel of a Bushmaster, part of a convoy.

A largely pointless conflict that receded deeper into his consciousness as the years went by, the crimes he had committed since helping cauterise his memories of the war.

Watching through the night vision goggles, however, Chance was reminded of the time a bomb had been detonated outside the base. A loud bang, immediately followed by the whoosh of Taliban rocket and mortar fire. He remembered the cacophony of noise from the resulting explosions, the local Afghans going crazy, the crackle of radio communications, the screams of a soldier with a piece of shrapnel in his leg. Chance had spent a tense night scanning the perimeter through similar goggles to the ones he had now, the flat ground leading up to the wire lit up in a spectral green.

He'd heard the stories, always told *sotto voce*, about groups like the Special Forces, the kill boards they pinned on the barracks doors, the deliberate blooding of junior members into the raw business of killing. He'd just driven trucks, had spent that night terrified, willing himself to do what would have to be done if the Taliban swarmed across the wire. The same emotions coursed through him now.

Chance consulted his watch, figured the tall man and his party had turned in for the night. Now or never. He went over the plan one more time with Eva and Loomis.

'You sure you both know what to do?'

'Yes,' Eva said. She reached for the jerry can in front of her, the petrol sloshing around as she picked it up. 'Fifteen minutes, then I blow it.'

''What about you, old man?

'Quite sure.' He cocked the Sten theatrically. '"Once more unto the breach, dear friends, once more".'

'Good luck.'

ELEVEN

Chance grabbed the tyre iron and sprinted the distance from the tree line to the orphanage building, hoping like hell he was right about the cellar doors. He blinked, breathed deeply, and looked down. The wooden doors were old, secured by a rusty link of chain wrapped around two wooden handles.

Using the tyre iron as a lever, Chance easily prized one of the handles away, nails coming out of the rotting wood like it was putty.

Chance opened the cellar door and was assailed by a damp musty odour as he peered into the blackness. Withdrawing the Luger, he flipped the googles down over his eyes and turned them on. A set of stone stairs materialised before him.

He descended into a room crammed with junk, broken furniture, wooden crates, piles of bottles, old farm tools. He was making his way to a door at the far end of the room when he heard a groan. He followed the sound until he came across a figure lying on a mattress.

Ripped from the familiarity of her usual surrounds, without makeup, it took Chance a moment to recognise Leigh. Her face, much older, looked as if it belonged to someone else. The wrinkled skin was streaked with grime, her thinning hair dank and matted. Her bottom lip was cut, dried blood on her chin. Her left eye was surrounded by a dark bruise and almost swollen shut. She was clad in tracksuit pants and jumper, a filthy pair of runners on her feet.

'Please, for the love of God,' she said weakly. 'Help me.'

A length of rope, secured around one of her ankles, snaked across the dirt floor and was tied to a pipe that protruded from the brick wall. An old metal bucket sat next to the mattress, a foul smell emanating from it, along with a half empty plastic bottle of water and several chocolate wrappers.

Chance tucked the pistol into his jeans, bent down on one knee, and helped Leigh sit up.

'Vera, it's Chance.'

'Gary?' She looked up at him with her one good eye. 'Darling, you were always good at making an entrance.'

Leigh motioned towards the water.

Chance put the bottle to her lips.

'How did you know I was here?' she said in between sips.

'I didn't. You just got lucky.'

'What about Loomis and Angel?'

'Angel's dead. Loomis is outside with Eva.'

'Dead...How?'

'Killed during your kidnapping. The shit you've caused, Vera. I ought to leave you here to fester in your own stench.'

'Gary, I'm so sorry, love. I swear, didn't mean all this to happen.'

'Save it for when we're out of this mess.' Chance pulled a pocketknife from the pocket of his denim jacket, opened the blade, and started cutting through the rope.

'Right now, I need you to tell me how many people are upstairs.'

'Hardigan. A big man, I think his name is Swain. His tramp, Celeste. And that little shit Tremont.'

'What can you tell me about Hardigan?'

'An ex-Jack. He's the one in charge but he's fucking crazy, knows about Mundy and the diamonds, will do anything to find them.'

'He's not the only one.'

He helped her up, roughly turned her in the direction of the cellar exit. 'That way is out. Go, but watch out for Loomis. He's been told to shoot at anything that moves.'

Tremont had never been so scared in his life.

He lay on top of the sleeping bag spread out on the wooden floorboards in the darkness. His arms ached from swinging a sledgehammer for most of the day. His skin was covered in plaster dust, and the musty decay of the building filled his nostrils.

He'd been relieved at first when Hardigan walked into Mudcrab's house and told them about some guy called Mundy who'd escaped with millions in diamonds from a heist half a century ago. Hardigan said he was an ex-cop, looking for the stones ever since the robbery. He made everyone in the room a proposition: help him in return for a share of whatever they recovered.

Tremont hadn't believed any of it but hoped it would at least distract Swain and the others from engaging in their own little Night of the Long Knives with him as the target, giving him some time to figure out how to escape.

But things had got only worse. Hardigan was obsessed with finding the diamonds. The death of the Mundy woman, kidnapping Leigh, now ripping apart this creepy old building. He was prepared to do anything.

And the way he'd knocked Mudcrab, right in front of them, with no more remorse than swatting a fly. Not that Tremont wasn't relieved the little scumbag was out of the picture. But the stone-cold look in the old man's eyes after he'd shot him said he'd do the same to anyone who got in his way.

Tremont and Swain had buried Mudcrab's body in a shallow grave near the one they had dug for Sylvia Mundy.

He listened to Hardigan snoring unevenly in the next room. The ex-cop had sweated Leigh, got a tale out of her about how she'd dumped her child here, then the rumour Mundy, like an avenging ghost, had emerged from wherever he'd been hiding to rescue the kid and exact retribution on the priest who'd abused him.

When the priest had backed up the story, Hardigan became convinced with the ridiculous idea the diamonds, or at least evidence of their real location, was stashed somewhere in this building. They'd spent most of the day demolishing the insides, overseen by the increasingly erratic ex-cop. But all they'd found were rodent carcasses, beer cans, old newspapers and used condoms.

They slept in small rooms off a long hallway on the second storey. Swain and Celeste shared the one on his left, Hardigan was in the room to his right. Tremont knew the front door of the orphanage wasn't locked and now was his chance. All he had to do was summon up the courage to make a run for it.

Swain still seemed to be on board with Hardigan's plan. The whiff of money for his fucked-up, right wing *Übermensch* revolution enough for now.

Celeste was starting to appear less enthusiastic. Maybe it was just her adverse reaction to a hard day of physical labour, never her strong suit. Tremont couldn't tell and didn't want to risk asking her.

Tremont took a deep breath and rose to his feet as quietly as possible. He fumbled for his shoes, hugging them to his chest with one hand, willing himself to put one foot in front of the other. He paused as one of the old boards groaned under his weight, listened for any movement in the rooms on either side of his, then continued when no one stirred.

He was feeling his way down the length of the hallway with an outstretched hand when the silence was ripped apart by a loud noise. The corridor shook and a crack between the sheet of corrugated tin and the window it covered near him lit up bright orange.

It took him a few seconds to register the sound was an explosion. Tremont gripped the wall, heart pounding in his chest.

Another blast followed. A torch light came on in Hardigan's room. 'What the hell is going on?' he yelled.

'How the fuck am I supposed to know?' Swain growled in reply.

Tremont knew he didn't have time to make it to the stairs before either Swain or Hardigan emerged from their rooms and caught him trying to escape. He felt for the nearest doorway, threw himself inside in the hope he'd be lost in the chaos.

'The cars,' barked Hardigan. 'It's the bloody cars. Go and find out what the bloody hell is happening, Swain, while I check downstairs.'

Tremont heard more swearing, then two pairs of heavy footfalls moving past the doorway, along with flashing torchlights. He waited until the sound had disappeared before stepping into the corridor.

He stood there wondering what to do when a light shone in his face.

'Carl?' said Celeste, lowering her torch.

Tremont froze, unsure what to do.

'What's going on, Carl? I'm scared.' She was dressed in a T-shirt and white underwear, looked at him imploringly.

The angry white nationalist of a few days ago seemed to have evaporated, replaced by the scared hippy girl he remembered rescuing her from the New Atlantis compound. He took a moment to try and assess whether it was a trick or if she was genuine.

'Put some clothes on,' he said. 'We're getting out of here.'

Chance heard the muffled blast as he entered what had once been a kitchen.

Most of the fixtures and fittings had been removed, an outline on the floor where a stove once stood. An ancient-looking fridge sat in a corner. Its door lay on the ground several metres away. Next to it sat a black plastic bag overflowing with fresh garbage.

The plan was for the explosion to drive some of the opposition into the path of Loomis's Sten. Chance just had to hope the old man had the mettle to take things from there.

He peered around the doorway into the next room. Two tattered armchairs positioned in front of an empty stone fireplace. More garbage, recently discarded beer cans lay on the floor around the armchairs, along with several cardboard boxes and a collection of sledgehammers and crowbars leaning against a wall.

An ascending wooden stair, the bannister broken in several places, ran along one side of the room, a passage underneath led into the darkness. Chance heard steps, watched Swain as he reached the bottom of the stairs.

Chance raised the Luger to fire, but Swain disappeared into the passage before he could let off a shot.

Chance stepped in the same direction when he heard more people moving about above him.

Chance hid behind one of the armchairs, waited until the footsteps had reached the bottom of the stairs, then stood, holding the Luger in both hands in front of him.

Celeste's torch beam briefly illuminated Chance aiming a gun at them before she dropped it and screamed. Standing next to her, Tremont, terrified, threw his hands in the air.

Tremont lowered his hands slightly, peered at the figure in the darkness. 'Is that you, Chance?'

Chance moved around the chair and strode towards them. 'Either of you armed?'

'What?' said Tremont. 'Shit, no.'

Chance lowered his gun, flipped the goggles up.

Celeste picked up the torch, smiled. 'Hi Gary,' she said sheepishly.

'What are you two doing?'

'We're getting the hell out of dodge. What does it look like?' hissed Tremont. 'Celeste said there is a back exit through the cellar. Which is cool with me because I am dead keen not to bump into Swain or that crazy old bastard Hardigan.'

'It's your lucky day, Carl. Go, and you better hope I never

lay eyes on you again.'

'*Ciao* buddy, the feeling's mutual.'

Eva crouched behind a large clump of bushes, felt the intense heat on her face as she watched the fire hungrily devour both vehicles.

As instructed, she had doused the four-wheel-drive in petrol, prised open the fuel cap on the van, stuffed a petrol-soaked cloth in and set it alight. She'd hardly had time to retreat to safety before the van exploded, the force of the blast almost pushing her over. The vehicle jumped several metres off the ground, sending flames into the night, landed on its side next to the four-wheel drive which followed suit soon after.

Her part in Chance's planned trap for those inside the building over, she didn't move. The blaze lit the orphanage building and a large circle of ground around it in rich Halloween orange.

Minutes passed and the wooden doors of the orphanage remained closed. Eva was contemplating her next move when she heard movement behind her. She turned to see Swain emerge from the shadows into the firelight, a gun pointed at her.

'Surprise.' The flames danced on his face.

She glanced between Swain and the orphanage, and saw the front doors were still closed.

'You didn't think I'd be stupid enough to just come barreling out the front? Nah, I took one of the metal sheets off the windows, came around the back way.' His mouth broke into a sadistic grin. 'I've been looking forward to meeting you again, Lilith.'

'I wish I could say the feeling was mutual.'

Eva reached for the knife in her boot, only got halfway before Swain let off a shot. She was aware of a numbness washing over her upper body, followed by an intense pain. She was suddenly looking up at the night, embers from the blazing cars floating across the sky in front of her. Swain stepped into view, looking down at her over the barrel of his gun. Then everything went black.

* * *

Swain was still standing over Eva's body when Loomis stepped out from between a clump of eucalypts, his face a mask of fierce determination. He held the Sten waist high, fired as he walked. Swain didn't even have time to see where death was coming from as the bullets made him do a little dance before throwing him backwards onto the ground.

'"When beggars die, there are no comets seen",' said Loomis. He quickly checked there was no life in the big man's tattered figure, before attending to Eva.

Loomis faltered slightly at the sight of her lying like a broken doll, open-eyed. His arms felt heavy. A tear ran down his cheek and he had to struggle to breathe through the tightness in his chest.

He wasn't sure how long he'd be standing there, surrounded by the dead, when he noticed something in the corner of his vision. Maybe an animal disturbed by the fire or another of Swain's crew. At the thought of the latter, Loomis fumbled with the Sten, brought it up in time to see a person walking towards him, the shape, weaving almost as if they'd had too much to drink, silhouetted against the fire.

Loomis raised the Sten, aimed, was about to fire, when Leigh came into focus.

Chance crept along a narrow hallway, doorways to small rooms at regular intervals along one side. Much of the old plaster on the walls was torn away to expose the strips of brittle wood underneath and lay in jagged strips on the floor.

He heard gun fire outside, two single shots, followed by a burst of Loomis's Sten.

Chance paused, waited for more shooting.

Someone approached from around the corner at the end of the hallway. Whoever it was held a torch, the beam dancing on the cracked wall ahead of them.

'Tremont, Celeste, where are you?' The unfamiliar voice sounded harsh, like the speaker was giving an order. Hardigan.

'They torched the bloody cars, and I can't find Swain anywhere.'

Chance stepped into one of the rooms and stood in the darkness, tried to breath as quietly as possible.

The glow from the flashlight turned into the hallway, came closer. It passed Chance's doorway, Hardigan following behind it.

'Jesus,' Hardigan said and froze as Chance stepped out and placed the barrel of the Luger gently against his temple.

The night vision goggles showed a gaunt face set at a determined angle. Hardigan's shoulders were ramrod straight, almost like he was at attention, a spectral soldier back from the afterlife to wreak revenge.

Hardigan let his pistol drop to the floor, swivelled his head without moving the rest of his body. He stared into the dark where he thought Chance's face was with eyes that were deep pools of fierce blackness.

'More than enough here for everyone, mate,' Hardigan said.

Chance squeezed the trigger and blew the top of Hardigan's head off.

TWELVE

The vehicles were still burning brightly as Chance emerged from the front entrance of the orphanage building, his hands in the air in front of him. He yelled his name in case Loomis was still on the lookout and inclined to shoot.

He found the old man sitting on a rock, smoking a joint.

'I said I'd stay clean until the end of the job,' Loomis said belligerently to no one in particular. 'I don't know about you, but it feels like the end of the job to me.'

Leigh sat on the dirt near him, her body almost bent over double, sobbing.

Eva was laid out on the ground in front of them, Swain's equally lifeless form sprawled a few metres away.

Chance forced himself to look at Eva, felt anger more than sorrow. Someone, probably Loomis, had closed her eyelids and placed her hands on her chest. Her clothes were dark with blood.

Chance rolled himself a cigarette as he listened to Loomis's curt summation of the events leading to Eva's death. Chance replied in kind.

'Where's Tremont and that girl, Celeste?' Loomis said when he was finished.

Chance lit his cigarette, inhaled deeply. 'If they're smart, as far away from here as possible.' He glared at Vera. She saw the look, winced like she'd been pricked with a needle.

'I swear, I didn't mean for any of this to happen.' Leigh shook off a rush of tears, sucked in breath as she glanced between the two men. 'Jamie, he was my boy, too. I just wanted to see him again. I just wanted to get my boy back. It's been so, so long...'

She paused as giant sobs wracked her body.

'Since you made the journey here, dropped Jamie off at these very doors?' said Chance, finishing her sentence.

She nodded, wiping tears away with the back of her hand.

Loomis placed a hand gently on Leigh's shoulder, left it there as he passed her the joint.

She took a hit, exhaled, then another, passed it back to Loomis.

'Where there ever any diamonds?' Chance said.

'At first, yes. Well, maybe. Jesus, Gary, I don't know. George said there were, but George said a lot of things. He said he'd only be overseas for a few months when he left Australia, just until things cooled down. That then he'd come back, leave his wife and we could be together.

'I couldn't blame him for fucking off, would've been a death sentence if he'd stayed. The cops, the crims, they'd all heard about the diamonds. From him or someone else, I can't even remember where the story originally came from, it was so long ago.

'I was pregnant with Jamie when he left, had him while George was gone. I waited but never heard anything from George. After a while I started to think, maybe the stories were right, that he was either dead or had just buggered off for good. I'd just opened the S&M dungeon and life was wild. The drink, the drugs, the parties. It was no place for a child, and I was in no condition most of the time to look after him.

'I didn't think of him for years, didn't know about what had happened at the orphanage.' She paused, fat tears running down her cheeks, breathed deeply. 'Until a year or so ago, when George's daughter, Sylvia, reached out to me. Her mum was dying, and she'd mentioned me as one of her father's friends from the time of the robbery. Sylvia had also heard the rumours about the diamonds, and when Grove died, she thought it might finally be safe to start looking. She asked me whether I might be able to help her track her father and the stones down.'

'Did she know just how friendly you'd been with her dad.'

'I don't think so. At first, I think I wanted to help her because I felt guilty.'

'Come off it, Vera, are you seriously telling me the possibility of finding the diamonds wasn't a consideration?' Chance dropped the butt of his cigarette, ground it out under the heel of his boot, as if to emphasise his point.

'Yeah, okay, there was that too.' A hint of defiance crept into her voice. 'My business was in the toilet. I needed the money. But then I started thinking about Jamie, that if I found George, maybe I could see my boy again.'

'And you told all this to Hardigan?'

'I had to tell him something,' she said pleadingly. 'He was crazy as a shithouse rat, was going to kill me whatever happened, I was sure of it. I just had to play for more time in the hope someone...you, Gary, would figure out where I was, come and get me.'

'Sylvia's dead too, you know that.'

Leigh's lower lip quivered as she nodded.

'One last thing I'm curious about. The rumours about Mundy being a spy. Were they true?'

'In Vietnam, yes. Afterwards, I have no idea. George cultivated an air of mystery, used to joke it helped him pull the birds. Well, it worked on me.'

Leigh stared at Eva's body lifeless in front of her, her eyes wide, as if she was seeing the corpse for the first time.

'I'm so sorry, Gary,' she said haltingly. 'I swear I never meant for all this to happen. You've got to believe me. Really. I'm getting out of the S&M business. I'm too old and the internet's changed it too much. I was going to accept the offer the developer had made for my business. I was just stalling until they upped the price, then I was going to cut you, the girl, and Loomis in for a slice.'

'Believe me, Vera, if there's one thing you're going to do, it's that,' Chance said over his shoulder as he walked off in the direction of the orphanage.

Chance found an old shovel among the farm tools in the cellar and working in the dying light of the burning vehicles, buried Eva in the graveyard next to the headstone of a thirteen-year-old boy who had died of influenza nearly a hundred years earlier. As he worked, Chance consoled himself Eva would feel at home among the other orphans.

RED DIRT AND
WIDE-OPEN SKY

ONE

At Loomis's suggestion, they dumped Hardigan and Swain's bodies in the cellar of the orphanage and set fire to the building. The blaze opened a large, pulsating red crack in the steel blue dawn horizon behind them as they drove back along Orphan Road.

They dropped Leigh off in Ballarat. A lot of things had come into Chance's mind to say to her, but none of them would bring Eva back or make any difference to what had happened.

'You'll be fine, Vera,' Chance said, as he ushered out of the car and stood on the footpath next to her, rolling a cigarette. 'You always are.' He passed her the cigarette, forced himself to look her in the eyes as he lit it for her. 'Take care of yourself.'

'You too, Gary.'

He and Loomis drove to the address on the driver's licence Chance found in a wallet in the orphanage room where Hardigan had been sleeping. It turned out to be an isolated farmhouse on a rolling stretch of fenced off land two hundred kilometres away.

Amid a thick grove of eucalypts on the southern edge of the property, they discovered two fresh graves, left them alone. Closer to the house, amid a well-tended flower garden, stood a waist high rectangular block of black marble—according to the gold letters on the headstone, the final resting place of Kieu Hardigan.

A hand-tinted enamel portrait filled a polished oval set in the face of the marble. The same slim, fine-featured woman appeared in a framed photograph as part of a small shrine sitting against a wall in a bedroom in the farmhouse, along with a cup containing the remains of several incense sticks and a small bowl of sweets and aging fruit.

Framed photographs lined the living room mantlepiece. The woman, always laughing; Hardigan, stern faced in various uniforms. Chance tried to imagine the two of them together but couldn't join the dots.

In a shed beside the house, Loomis found a file box containing the results of Hardigan's four-decade plus private investigation into the Great Bookie Robbery, and the fate of George Mundy and the diamonds: crime scene photographs and mug shots of the main players in the heist, pilfered police reports, decades of clipped newspaper and magazine articles. The *pièce de résistance*, a thick black notebook, page after page of spidery writing recording Hardigan's own scattered thoughts and observations about the case.

Chance and Loomis spent the night drinking Hardigan's single malt, the only luxury it appeared the man had allowed himself and reading all the material.

By dawn, they had culled the files and put together a list of possible leads in the search for Mundy. When they finished, they dumped everything Hardigan had collected into a brick incinerator in the backyard, doused it in kerosene and set it on fire.

After a few hours of sleep, they ransacked the house for provisions and money, and took off in the Ford Falcon. Their unspoken agreement: the need to do penance for Eva's death, and an even greater desire to put as much distance between them and Leigh, the orphanage, and the events of the last few months, as possible.

They took their time, lost themselves in the never-ending red dirt and wide-open skies of western New South Wales. Their first stop was the mining town of Broken Hill, where they spent the night in the company of an aging underworld hitman who lived in a caravan on a sun blasted patch of dirt on the outskirts of town.

The man had a voice like two pieces of sandpaper being rubbed together and expressionless eyes that, despite the heat, chilled Chance whenever he looked directly into them, as if they reflected his future. Chance and Loomis were woken in the middle of the night by the sound of their host prowling the perimeter of his property, armed with an old SLR rifle, and shouting orders to an imaginary platoon of soldiers, ghosts of the men he had commanded in Vietnam.

Based on what the hitman told them, they drove across the border into South Australia. After a morning spent digging up a yard in an abandoned house on the fringe of a small town, they excavated a steel chest containing several pistols, stripped-down parts for two submachine guns, a pair of handcuffs, a makeup kit and several wigs, everything bagged in plastic.

'Have you wondered why Hardigan collected all this information about the robbery but never seemed to follow any of it up?' Chance said as he picked over the trunk's contents.

'Maybe he was waiting for the one bit of information that would put the pieces together for him,' said Loomis, leaning on his shovel. 'Or perhaps he was just obsessed with the hunt.'

'Or just completely unhinged.'

'That's a possibility, too.'

With the information from Hardigan's files, they criss-crossed southeastern Australia. They followed up tips that didn't pan out, tracked down contacts who'd moved on, disappeared, died and, in one case, hadn't existed at all. Ex-cops, criminals, men and women who had played roles, large and small, in the fading criminal milieu of seventies Melbourne. Most wouldn't talk. Those that did often made no sense or had nothing of value to say.

Long days on the road, nights spent drinking in bars full of gruff, sunburned men who kept to themselves and eyed Loomis and Chance with a mixture of suspicion and curiosity, like mechanics figuring on stripping parts from a broken engine.

They slept in a succession of cheap motel rooms. Loomis smoked weed while Chance drank cheap spirits straight from the bottle, the television always left on, the volume low, a background thrum to their faltering conversations and long silences.

At some point, Chance stopped shaving. The beard, threaded with whisps of white, made him even more unrecognisable. Most nights he was plagued by a re-occurring nightmare of shooting Hardigan. The dream, always in night vision green, ended at the same point, the top of the man's head exploding, the tinkle of the bullet casing hitting the dusty floorboards at the exact same moment as the lifeless body.

Chance awoke one morning following a malaria relapse to find Loomis and the Falcon gone, leaving him alone in a threadbare room on the second storey of a pub in the speck of a town somewhere on the border between News South Wales and Queensland.

Chance tended bar in return for food and board, eventually finding his way into the bed of the blowsy female manager, whose own husband, the pub's owner, had disappeared several years ago, leaving her shackled to the business.

Chance was starting to wonder whether he could be happy here, just existing, when Loomis reappeared with a fresh lead.

The new information took them to a shack on a narrow strip of sand between the jungle and sea, almost to the very tip of northern Queensland, occupied by an elderly Filipino Australian man who had once made his living smuggling people and drugs between Australia and Papua New Guinea.

For a price, the Filipino was happy to recall ferrying an Australian man from an island off the coast of New Guinea to Australia sometime in late nineteen eighty-seven.

The passenger hadn't called himself George Mundy, but the Filipino identified him from the photograph in the Philadelphia newspaper, the copy of which Chance still had in his jacket pocket. The square of paper had been folded and unfolded so many times it had to be held together with clear tape.

The Filipino remembered the man acted like he was uncertain about being home. The man had paid to stay with him in his house for several weeks. The arrangement turned into several months, during which time the man helped on the Filipino's boat.

The man never talked about his past, was reluctant to share any details about himself at all. One of the few things he did reveal was about the house he was going to live in, one that had belonged to his parents. When he left, the man gave the Filipino a page torn from a magazine, an address scrawled on it, told him to visit if he was ever passing through. The Filipino sold it to Loomis and Chance for five hundred dollars.

They drove back along the coast, headed inland just before the border of Victoria and New South Wales, until they got to a small, neatly laid town on the banks of the olive-green water of the Murray River.

The address on the torn piece of paper was a single-storey brick house within eyeshot of two giant concrete grain silos. A row of Murray pines almost completely obscured the front of the house from the road. A narrow driveway, lined with thick bushes on either side, led to a side gate.

Chance waited until night had fallen before undoing the latch on the gate and letting himself in. He paused next to a giant bird of paradise plant in an overgrown back garden and spied a man sitting on a cane couch on the back porch. The man nursed a drink from a bottle from a small table in front of him.

His features were clearly visible in the glow from an overhead light, around which massed an army of insects. Half a century had aged the face from the one in the picture Chance still carried around. His skin was deeply tanned and his hair had turned snow white. But the man's features were unmistakably those of George Mundy.

Chance breathed deeply, his heart beating loudly in his ears, inhaled the scent of night jasmine mixed with rotting vegetation from the nearby riverbank. The blue light of a television was visible through one of the windows, the sound of canned laughter and applause mixing with the thrum of the cicadas as it drifted across the garden.

'You look pretty good for someone is supposed to be buried in a forest on the outskirts of Philadelphia,' Chance said as he emerged from the garden.

Mundy sipped his drink. If he was surprised by his unannounced nocturnal visitor, he didn't show it.

'Whoever you are,' Mundy said cautiously, 'it feels like I've been waiting for you for a long time.'

'And who could I be?' said Chance standing directly in front of him.

'The Mafia, the Agency, the police. They've all got long memories.' Mundy indicated with his glass at the bottle. 'Got time for a drink?'

Chance picked up the bottle. Bourbon. 'Got a taste for this in the US, did you?'

Mundy nodded as Chance sat in a matching cane chair.

'Jamie,' Mundy said over his shoulder.

A man appeared, pressed his face against a sliding fly wire screen door. He was middle-aged, a paunch visible under a faded black Star Wars T-shirt but had a boyish face despite the greying hair on his temples. He exuded a slightly shell-shocked countenance Chance recognised from his time in Afghanistan.

'Get me another glass, would you, mate?'

The man stared at Chance, hesitated.

'Don't worry, Jamie. Mister…I didn't catch your name?'

'Egan.'

'Mister Egan just dropped by with news about an old friend. He won't be staying long.'

'That your son, the one you took from the orphanage?' Chance asked when the younger man had gone.

'Yes. The things that priest did to him,' Mundy shook his

head. 'Still hasn't recovered. Nightmares, panic attacks. Gets nervous around strangers.'

'You got your payback.'

'That I did.' Mundy's eyes narrowed, and he smiled at their shared knowledge. 'Some days, though, reckon I should've just killed the prick.'

Mundy's son reappeared, placed a glass on the table. 'Our show starts soon, Dad,' he said with a slight falter, his eyes on Chance.

'I know Jamie,' said Mundy as he poured Chance a drink. 'Everything's okay, really. Go inside. I'll be along in a minute.'

'Will I be okay?' Mundy said when the son had gone back inside.

'Depends,' Chance replied softly, aware of the son hovering somewhere inside, just out of his field of vision.

'I don't have the diamonds, if that's what you are after.'

'I'm not your confessor, Mundy, or whatever you call yourself now.' Chance sipped his drink. 'And I don't want your war stories. I just want to know what happened.'

Mundy drained his drink and poured himself another, stared at his overgrown back garden for a beat before answering.

'The diamonds had been smuggled from Apartheid South Africa into Melbourne on the way to Manila, where they were going to be used to finance some of the CIA's post-Vietnam War hijinks. I don't know what. They were being held by a friendly bookie who used to lend a hand with the Agency's money laundering in Australia. That counting room would've been safe as houses, if not for the fact that Chuck Bennett and his gang picked just that time to heist the joint.'

'Had you been working for the CIA for a while?'

'On and off since I'd been with the Australian Army Training Team in Vietnam. It wasn't unusual. Back in the day, seemed like every second person in Vietnam was on the Agency's payroll one way or another. I continued working as an independent contractor after I came back to Australia. Months went by when I'd hear nothing, then out of the blue there was a call. Whenever Langley had trouble with the locals. Low-level stuff mostly.'

'And they called you after the Great Bookie Robbery?'

'The Agency boys had fucking puppies when they heard the stones had been pinched along with the cash in the robbery.' Mundy chuckled at the memory. 'They asked me to help get them back. Melbourne was a smaller place then. The criminal world was even smaller, everyone knew everyone.

'I'd met Bennett, was able to contact him. He had enough on his plate with the cops and other crims trying to muscle in on the take from the robbery. And he was smart enough to know the stones were hot as hell. There was no way he could safely move them himself. I offered my help for a price.'

'And your friends in the Painters and Dockers got you a ratline out of the country.'

'Yes, a boat to Manila.'

'What happened then?'

'Cooled my heels for a while until I got a phone call, told me to be at a certain bar at a certain time, with the stones.'

'Groves's bar?'

'The one and only. I'm sitting at the counter, drinking an ice-cold San Miguel, a backpack with the diamonds at my feet, thinking how strange it was that none of the girls working the joint that night would come anywhere near me. It was like that night I was a ghost.

'Eventually, a man walks in a safari suit and dark sunglasses, sits on the bar stool next to mine. I could tell he was a Langley boy, square jawed, crew cut. The bartender nods to me, my signal to go to the toilet. When I came back, the man and the backpack are gone and there's an envelope full of cash lying on the bar next to my half-finished beer.'

'Mission accomplished,' said Chance, raising his glass in a mock toast.

'Yeah, only by then my name was on the lips of every criminal and cop on the eastern seaboard of Australia. I would've been knocked just like that had I come back. Didn't much want to anyway, truth be told. Took me a while to realise it, but the night I fled Melbourne it wasn't just the cops I was running from. It was the wife I'd married too young, the child I hadn't expected. My whole damn life. I wasn't cut out to be a husband or a father, not then, anyway. I know it was a complete bastard of a move, but reckon I did Ruthie and Sylvia a favour pissing off out of their lives.'

'I'm not sure they saw it like that.'

'Besides, I still send them money, look after them in my own way.'

Chance realised Mundy wasn't aware his wife and daughter were dead.

'So, I drifted. Did some work for the Agency in Bangkok and Hong Kong. One thing led to another, and I ended up in Philadelphia, looking after some of the CIA's narcotics interests. Don't get me wrong, any enthusiasm I had for the Agency's political agenda had quickly evaporated after Vietnam. This was just survival, an any port in a storm kind of thing.'

'And your boy, is he why you came back to Australia?'

'I'd like to say yes, but the truth is, things were getting hot for me in Philly. I was skimming from the Mob's heroin operations. But I was also sick of the whole scene, the drugs, the junkies, the Mob guys, my CIA handlers, who seemed to get younger and stupider each year.'

'You arranged to die?'

'Yeah, took some doing too, let me tell you.'

'Out of curiosity, who is buried under that shopping mall in the forest?'

'A low-level mob enforcer by the name of Francisco Rossi. He was a pimp and a wife beater. Believe me, no one missed him, least of all his missus. Anyway, I'd been back about six months when the urge to see my son came on strong.'

'You could've just asked the boy's mother where he was?'

'What, Vera?' Mundy chuckled deeply. 'I'd barely got out of

Philly alive, and there were still people looking for me in Melbourne. I meant what I said about wanting to stay out of the life, and Vera wasn't exactly low profile in those days. If I'd contacted her, I may as well have taken out a full-page newspaper ad announcing I was back.'

Mundy read the scepticism on Chance's face. 'But, yeah, the subterfuge and secrets, you live them long enough, they become habit forming, hard to break. Besides, with my skills, it wasn't hard finding which orphanage Jamie was in and what went on there.'

Mundy refilled Chance's glass.

'Listen, I don't know who you are, and I don't want to know. My boy, I'm all he has. I don't have a lot of money, but what I have, I'll give you to leave me alone and help me stay forgotten.'

Chance picked up his drink, stared into the amber liquid. He was suddenly aware of the grip of the Luger digging into the small of his back.

'A lot of people are dead because of you, George.'

'Did I ask any of them to follow me and the diamonds?' Mundy said and sipped his drink. 'I just want to be left alone.'

The sound of the television and the thrum of the cicadas was interrupted by the clank of a freight train somewhere in the distance.

Chance withdrew the burner phone from his jeans pocket as he exited Mundy's driveway and brought up Leigh's number. He keyed Mundy's address into a text message, pressed send.

He kept walking until he found a roadside stormwater drain, dropped the phone into its mouth, the Luger after it.

Loomis, in the driver's seat of the Ford Falcon, turned to Chance as he slid in next to him, one of his thick eyebrows raised. The Clash, *London's Calling*, was playing on the car stereo and the interior smelt of the joint Loomis smoked while he was waiting.

'Let's roll, old man.'

Chance filled Loomis in as they drove through the empty streets, picking up speed as the car turned onto the stretch of blacktop heading out of town.

The night outside swirled and churned with the angry ghosts they'd conjured over the past months. Chance knew they wouldn't be able to shake them, no matter how far they drove.

ANDREW NETTE is the author of two previous novels, *Ghost Money* and *Gunshine State*. He is the co-editor of three books on the history of post war pulp and popular fiction, all published by PM Press, the most recent of which, *Dangerous Visions and New Worlds: Radical Science Fiction, 1950-1985* appeared in late 2021. His writing on film, books and culture has also appeared in a variety of print and on-line publications. You can find him at his website, PulpCurry.com and on Twitter at @Pulpcurry.

BOOKS

On the following pages are a few
more great titles from the
Down & Out Books publishing family.

For a complete list of books and to
sign up for our newsletter,
go to DownAndOutBooks.com.

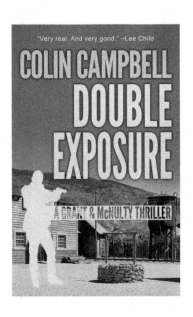

Double Exposure
A Grant & McNulty Thriller
Colin Campbell

Down & Out Books
April 2023
978-1-64396-309-9

Titanic Productions is filming on a movie ranch near Los Angeles when Jim Grant pays a visit. A drug cartel that both Grant and McNulty have crossed paths with has tried to kill Grant's brother in Shelter Cove and is now after McNulty's sister. And her daughter. After a shootout at Nantasket Peninsula, Grant and McNulty decide to take the fight to the cartel. Their tactics include a pizza truck, a prison break and the FBI. And one last chance to print the legend.

"No one writes better action sequences than Campbell." —Dana King, author of the Penns River and Shamus-nominated Nick Forte novels

Splintered Loyalty
An Ava Rome Mystery
Mark Troy

Down & Out Books
May 2023
978-1-64396-311-2

A World War II cold case and a domestic violence case combine to pit Honolulu private eye Ava Rome in a dangerous struggle against a powerful, violent organization that wants the past to remain secret.

Ava's quest takes her to the remains of the Tule Lake internment camp on a dangerous mission to find the killer of a Buddhist priest and a Japanese-American teenager.

"Ava Rome, is tough, talented and tenacious and riveting to watch! Bravo!" —Matt Coyle, author of the Shamus, Anthony and Lefty Award-winning Rick Cahill crime series

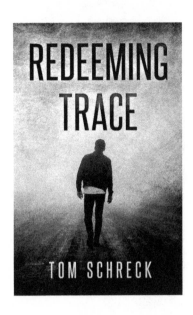

Redeeming Trace
Tom Schreck

Down & Out Books
May 2023
978-1-64396-312-9

Fresh out of graduate school, CIA psychologist, Trace Curran works his dream job providing trauma-based psychotherapy and researching the threat level of Antifa-based organizations.

While domestic terror escalates, Trace's world is rocked, when an agent on his caseload commits a murder-suicide.

When the terrorism turns towards him he must face his fears and save everything that is important to him.

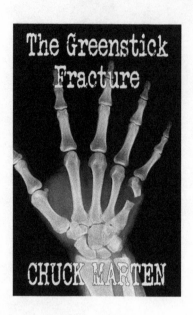

The Greenstick Fracture
Chuck Marten

Down & Out Books
May 2023
978-1-64396-314-3

After one drink too many, hapless medical student Edwin Greenstick wakes up with a broken hand and no memory of the night before.

Next thing he knows, Edwin is accused of stealing from the mob and implicated in the disappearance of a murder witness.

Piecing together what happened will require a quick wit and a cool head. Regrettably, Edwin has neither of those qualities.